continued . . .

"The Telling is a signal event in recent SF history . . . the first full-length novel in Le Guin's much-honored Hainish cycle since *The Dispossessed* more than a quarter-century ago . . . As always, Le Guin is wise, judicious, elegant, and *The Telling* is in may ways the mature expression of what nearly all her fiction has tended toward . . . a peerless maker of tales."
—Gary K. Wolfe, *Locus*

"Ursula K. Le Guin's prose breathes light and intelligence. She can lift fiction to the level of poetry and compress it to the density of allegory—in *The Telling* she does both gorgeously."
—Jonathan Lethem, author of *Motherless Brooklyn*

"On the individual level of memories, hopes, sorrows, *The Telling* is a powerfully moving book. It also works in a much broader perspective, offering insights into the many facets of religion, for both good and evil, that are thoroughly relevant to our times. This is humanist SF at its best, Le Guin in top form."
—Faren Miller, *Locus*

"Le Guin has long been a master of literary science fiction that is both thoughtful and thought-provoking. This novel in her Hainish cycle, which includes *The Word for World is Forest*, *The Left Hand of Darkness*, and *The Dispossessed*, is no exception . . . Aka and its society, past and present, are impressively visualized, as are Sutty's internalization and slow grasp of what she is seeking."
—*Booklist*

Ace Books by
Ursula K. Le Guin

The Left Hand of Darkness
The Telling

URSULA K. LE GUIN

THE Telling

ACE BOOKS, NEW YORK

THE TELLING

An Ace Book / published by arrangement with
Harcourt, Inc.

PRINTING HISTORY
Harcourt hardcover edition / 2000
Ace trade paperback edition / October 2001

Visit our website at
www.penguinputnam.com

Check our the ACE Science Fiction & Fantasy newsletter
and much more on the Internet at Club PPI!

Library of Congress Cataloging-in-Publication Data

Le Guin, Ursula K., 1929–
The telling / Ursula K. Le Guin.
p. cm.
ISBN 0-441-00863-1 (alk. paper)
I. Title.
PS3562.E42 T45 2001
813'.54—dc21
2001022150

ACE®
Ace Books are published by The Berkley Publishing Group,
a division of Penguin Putnam Inc., 375 Hudson Street,
New York, New York 10014.
ACE and the "A" design are trademarks
belonging to Penguin Putnam Inc.

PRINTED IN THE UNITED STATES OF AMERICA

10 9 8 7 6 5 4 3 2 1

The day I was born I made my first mistake,

and by that path

have I sought wisdom ever since.

THE MAHABHARATA

U N E

WHEN SUTTY WENT back to Earth in the daytime, it was always to the village. At night, it was the Pale.

Yellow of brass, yellow of turmeric paste and of rice cooked with saffron, orange of marigolds, dull orange haze of sunset dust above the fields, henna red, passionflower red, dried-blood red, mud red: all the colors of sunlight in the day. A whiff of asafetida. The brook-babble of Aunty gossiping with Moti's mother on the verandah. Uncle Hurree's dark hand lying still on a white page. Ganesh's little piggy kindly eye. A match struck and the rich grey curl of incense smoke: pungent, vivid, gone. Scents, glimpses, echoes that drifted or glimmered through her mind when she was walking the

streets, or eating, or taking a break from the sensory assault of
the neareals she had to partiss in, in the daytime, under the
other sun.

But night is the same on any world. Light's absence is
only that. And in the darkness, it was the Pale she was in. Not
in dream, never in dream. Awake, before she slept, or when
she woke from dream, disturbed and tense, and could not get
back to sleep. A scene would begin to happen, not in sweet,
bright bits but in full recall of a place and a length of time;
and once the memory began, she could not stop it. She had
to go through it until it let her go. Maybe it was a kind of punishment, like the lovers' punishment in Dante's Hell, to
remember being happy. But those lovers were lucky, they
remembered it together.

The rain. The first winter in Vancouver rain. The sky like
a roof of lead weighing down on the tops of buildings, flat-
tening the huge black mountains up behind the city. Southward the rain-rough grey water of the Sound, under which
lay Old Vancouver, drowned by the sea rise long ago. Black
sleet on shining asphalt streets. Wind, the wind that made
her whimper like a dog and cringe, shivering with a scared
exhilaration, it was so fierce and crazy, that cold wind out of
the Arctic, ice breath of the snow bear. It went right through
her flimsy coat, but her boots were warm, huge ugly black
plastic boots splashing in the gutters, and she'd soon be
home. It made you feel safe, that awful cold. People hurried
past not bothering each other, all their hates and passions

frozen. She liked the North, the cold, the rain, the beautiful, dismal city.

Aunty looked so little, here, little and ephemeral, like a small butterfly. A red-and-orange cotton saree, thin brass bangles on insect wrists. Though there were plenty of Indians and Indo-Canadians here, plenty of neighbors, Aunty looked small even among them, displaced, misplaced. Her smile seemed foreign and apologetic. She had to wear shoes and stockings all the time. Only when she got ready for bed did her feet reappear, the small brown feet of great character which had always, in the village, been a visible part of her as much as her hands, her eyes. Here her feet were put away in leather cases, amputated by the cold. So she didn't walk much, didn't run about the house, bustle about the kitchen. She sat by the heater in the front room, wrapped up in a pale ragged knitted woollen blanket, a butterfly going back into its cocoon. Going away, farther away all the time, but not by walking.

Sutty found it easier now to know Mother and Father, whom she had scarcely known for the last fifteen years, than to know Aunty, whose lap and arms had been her haven. It was delightful to discover her parents, her mother's good-natured wit and intellect, her father's shy, unhandy efforts at showing affection. To converse with them as an adult while knowing herself unreasonably beloved as a child—it was easy, it was delightful. They talked about everything, they learned one another. While Aunty shrank, fluttered away very softly, deviously, seeming not to be going anywhere, back to the village, to Uncle Hurree's grave.

Spring came, fear came. Sunlight came back north here long and pale like an adolescent, a silvery shadowy radiance. Small pink plum trees blossomed all down the side streets of the neighborhood. The Fathers declared that the Treaty of Beijing contravened the Doctrine of Unique Destiny and must be abrogated. The Pales were to be opened, said the Fathers, their populations allowed to receive the Holy Light, their schools cleansed of unbelief, purified of alien error and deviance. Those who clung to sin would be re-educated.

Mother was down at the Link offices every day, coming home late and grim. This is their final push, she said; if they do this, we have nowhere to go but underground.

In late March, a squadron of planes from the Host of God flew from Colorado to the District of Washington and bombed the Library there, plane after plane, four hours of bombing that turned centuries of history and millions of books into dirt. Washington was not a Pale, but the beautiful old building, though often closed and kept locked, under guard, had never been attacked; it had endured through all the times of trouble and war, breakdown and revolution, until this one. The Time of Cleansing. The Commander-General of the Hosts of the Lord announced the bombing while it was in progress, as an educational action. Only one Word, only one Book. All other words, all other books were darkness, error. They were dirt. *Let the Lord shine out!* cried the pilots in their white uniforms and mirror-masks, back at the church at Colorado Base, facelessly facing the cameras and the singing, swaying crowds in ecstasy. *Wipe away the filth and let the Lord shine out!*

But the new Envoy who had arrived from Hain last year, Dalzul, was talking with the Fathers. They had admitted Dalzul to the Sanctum. There were neareals and holos and 2Ds of him in the net and *Godsword.* It seemed that the Commander-General of the Hosts had not received orders from the Fathers to destroy the Library of Washington. The error was not the Commander-General's, of course. Fathers made no errors. The pilots' zeal had been excessive, their action unauthorised. Word came from the Sanctum: the pilots were to be punished. They were led out in front of the ranks and the crowds and the cameras, publicly stripped of their weapons and white uniforms. Their hoods were taken off, their faces were bared. They were led away in shame to re-education.

All that was on the net, though Sutty could watch it without having to partiss in it, Father having disconnected the vr-proprios. *Godsword* was full of it, too. And full of the new Envoy, again. Dalzul was a Terran. Born right here on God's Earth, they said. A man who understood the men of Earth as no alien ever could, they said. A man from the stars who came to kneel at the feet of the Fathers and to discuss the implementation of the peaceful intentions of both the Holy Office and the Ekumen.

"Handsome fellow," Mother said, peering. "What is he? A white man?"

"Inordinately so," Father said.

"Wherever is he from?"

But no one knew. Iceland, Ireland, Siberia, everybody had a different story. Dalzul had left Terra to study on Hain, they all agreed on that. He had qualified very quickly as an Observer, then as a Mobile, and then had been sent back home: the first Terran Envoy to Terra.

"He left well over a century ago," Mother said. "Before the Unists took over East Asia and Europe. Before they even amounted to much in Western Asia. He must find his world quite changed."

Lucky man, Sutty was thinking. Oh lucky, lucky man! He got away, he went to Hain, he studied at the School on Ve, he's been where everything isn't God and hatred, where they've lived a million years of history, where they understand it all!

That same night she told Mother and Father that she wanted to study at the Training School, to try to qualify for the Ekumenical College. Told them very timidly, and found them undismayed, not even surprised. "This seems a rather good world to get off of, at present," Mother said.

They were so calm and favorable that she thought, Don't they realise, if I qualify and get sent to one of the other worlds, they'll never see me again? Fifty years, a hundred, hundreds, round trips in space were seldom less, often more. Didn't they care? It was only later that evening, when she was watching her father's profile at table, full lips, hook nose, hair beginning to go grey, a severe and fragile face, that it occurred to her that if she was sent to another world, she would never see them again either. They had thought about it before she did. Brief presence and long absence, that was all she and they had ever had. And made the best of it.

"Eat, Aunty," Mother said, but Aunty only patted her piece of naan with her little ant-antenna fingers and did not pick it up.

"Nobody could make good bread with such flour," she said, exonerating the baker.

"You were spoiled, living in the village," Mother teased her. "This is the best quality anybody can get in Canada. Best quality chopped straw and plaster dust."

"Yes, I was spoiled," Aunty said, smiling from a far country.

———

The older slogans were carved into facades of buildings: FORWARD TO THE FUTURE. PRODUCER-CONSUMERS OF AKA MARCH TO THE STARS. Newer ones ran across the buildings in bands of dazzling electronic display: REACTIONARY THOUGHT IS THE DEFEATED ENEMY. When the displays malfunctioned, the messages became cryptic: OD IS ON.

The newest ones hovered in holopro above the streets: PURE SCIENCE DESTROYS CORRUPTION. UPWARD ONWARD FORWARD. Music hovered with them, highly rhythmic, multivoiced, crowding the air. "Onward, onward to the stars!" an invisible choir shrilled to the stalled traffic at the intersection where Sutty's robocab sat. She turned up the cab sound to drown the tune out. "Superstition is a rotting corpse," the sound system said in a rich, attractive male voice. "Superstitious practices defile youthful minds. It is the responsibility of every citizen, whether adult or student, to report reactionary teachings and to bring teachers who permit sedition or introduce irrationality and superstition in their classroom to the attention of the authorities. In the light of Pure Science we know that the ardent cooperation of all the people is the first requisite of—" Sutty turned the sound down as far as it would go. The choir burst forth, "To the stars! To the stars!" and the robocab jerked forward about half its length. Two more jerks and it might get through the intersection at the next flowchange.

Sutty felt in her jacket pockets for an akagest, but she'd eaten them all. Her stomach hurt. Bad food, she'd eaten too much bad food for too long, processed stuff jacked up with proteins, condiments, stimulants, so you had to buy the stupid akagests. And the stupid unnecessary traffic jams because the stupid badly made cars broke down all the time, and the noise all the time, the slogans, the songs, the hype, a people hyping itself into making every mistake every other population in FF-tech mode had ever made. —Wrong.

Judgmentalism. Wrong to let frustration cloud her thinking and perceptions. Wrong to admit prejudice. Look, listen,
notice: observe. That was her job. This wasn't her world.

But she was on it, in it, how could she observe it when
there was no way to back off from it? Either the hyperstimu-
lation of the neareals she had to study, or the clamor of the
streets: nowhere to get away from the endless aggression of
propaganda, except alone in her apartment, shutting out the
world she'd come to observe.

The fact was, she was not suited to be an Observer here.
In other words, she had failed on her first assignment. She
knew that the Envoy had summoned her to tell her so.

She was already nearly late for the appointment. The
robocab made another jerk forward, and its sound system
came up loud for one of the Corporation announcements
that overrode low settings. There was no off button. "An
announcement from the Bureau of Astronautics!" said a
woman's vibrant, energy-charged, self-confident voice, and
Sutty put her hands over her ears and shouted, "Shut up!"

"Doors of vehicle are closed," the robocab said in the flat
mechanical voice assigned to mechanisms responding to verbal orders. Sutty saw that this was funny, but she couldn't
laugh. The announcement went on and on while the shrill
voices in the air sang, "Ever higher, ever greater, marching to
the stars!"

The Ekumenical Envoy, a doe-eyed Chiffewarian named
Tong Ov, was even later than she for their appointment, hav-

ing been delayed at the exit of his apartment house by a mal-
function of the ZIL-screening system, which he laughed
about. "And the system here has mislaid the microrec I
wanted to give you," he said, going through files in his office.
"I coded it, because of course they go through my files, and
my code confused the system. But I know it's in here. . . . So,
meanwhile, tell me how things have been going."

"Well," Sutty said, and paused. She had been speaking
and thinking in Dovzan for months. She had to go through
her own files for a moment: Hindi no, English no, Hainish
yes. "You asked me to prepare a report on contemporary language and literature. But the social changes that took place
here while I was in transit . . . Well, since it's against the law,
now, to speak or study any language but Dovzan and Hainish,
I can't work on the other languages. If they still exist. As for
Dovzan, the First Observers did a pretty thorough linguistic
survey. I can only add details and vocabulary."

"What about literature?" Tong asked.

"Everything that was written in the old scripts has been
destroyed. Or if it exists, I don't know what it is, because the
Ministry doesn't allow access to it. So all I was able to work
on is modern aural literature. All written to Corporation
specifications. It tends to be very—to be standardised."

She looked at Tong Ov to see if her whining bored him,
but though still looking for the mislaid file, he seemed to be
listening with lively interest. He said, "All aural, is it?"

"Except for the Corporation manuals hardly anything's

printed, except printouts for the deaf, and primers to accompany sound texts for early learners. . . . The campaign against the old ideographic forms seems to have been very intense. Maybe it made people afraid to write—made them distrust writing in general. Anyway, all I've been able to get hold of by way of literature is sound tapes and neareals. Issued by the World Ministry of Information and the Central Ministry of Poetry and Art. Most of the works are actually information or educational material rather than, well, literature or poetry as I understand the terms. Though a lot of the neareals are dramatisations of practical or ethical problems and solutions. . . ." She was trying so hard to speak factually, unjudgmentally, without prejudice, that her voice was totally toneless.

"Sounds dull," said Tong, still flitting through files.

"Well, I'm, I think I'm insensitive to this aesthetic. It is so deeply and, and, and flatly political. Of course every art is political. But when it's *all* didactic, all in the service of a belief system, I resent, I mean, I resist it. But I try not to. Maybe, since they've essentially erased their history— Of course there was no way of knowing they were on the brink of a cultural revolution, at the time I was sent here— But anyhow, for this particular Observership, maybe a Terran was a bad choice. Given that we on Terra are living the future of a people who denied their past."

She stopped short, appalled at everything she had said.

Tong looked round at her, unappalled. He said, "I don't

wonder that you feel that what you've been trying to do can't be done. But I needed your opinion. So it was worth it to me. But tiresome for you. A change is in order." There was a gleam in his dark eyes. "What do you say to going up the river?"

"The river?"

"It's how they say 'into the backwoods,' isn't it? But in fact I meant the Ereha."

When he said the name, she remembered that a big river ran through the capital, partly paved over and so hidden by buildings and embankments that she couldn't remember ever having seen it except on maps.

"You mean go outside Dovza City?"

"Yes," Tong said. "Outside the city! And not on a guided tour! For the first time in fifty years!" He beamed like a child revealing a hidden present, a beautiful surprise. "I've been here two years, and I've put in eighty-one requests for permission to send a staff member to live or stay somewhere outside Dovza City or Kangnegne or Ert. Politely evaded, eighty times, with offers of yet another guided tour of the space-program facilities or the beauty of spring in the Eastern Isles. I put in such requests by habit, by rote. And suddenly one is granted! Yes! 'A member of your staff is authorised to spend a month in Okzat-Ozkat.' Or is it Ozkat-Okzat? It's a small city, in the foothills, up the river. The Ereha rises in the High Headwaters Range, about fifteen hundred kilos inland. I asked for that area, Rangma, never expecting to get it, and I got it!" He beamed.

"Why there?"

"I heard about some people there who sound interesting."

"An ethnic fragment population?" she asked, hopeful. Early in her stay, when she first met Tong Ov and the other two Observers presently in Dovza City, they had all discussed the massive monoculturalism of modern Aka in its large cities, the only places the very few offworlders permitted on the planet were allowed to live. They were all convinced that Akan society must have diversities and regional variations and frustrated that they had no way to find out.

"Sectarians, I suspect, rather than ethnic. A cult. Possibly remnants in hiding of a banned religion."

"Ah," she said, trying to preserve her expression of interest.

Tong was still searching his files. "I'm looking for the little I've gathered on the subject. Sociocultural Bureau reports on surviving criminal antiscientific cult activities. And also a few rumors and tales. Secret rites, walking on the wind, miraculous cures, predictions of the future. The usual."

To fall heir to a history of three million years was to find little in human behavior or invention that could be called unusual. Though the Hainish bore it lightly, it was a burden on their various descendants to know that they would have a hard time finding a new thing, even an imaginary new thing, under any sun.

Sutty said nothing.

"In the material the First Observers here sent to Terra," Tong pursued, "did anything concerning religions get through?"

"Well, since nothing but the language report came through undamaged, information about anything was pretty much only what we could infer from vocabulary."

"All that information from the only people ever allowed to study Aka freely—lost in a glitch," said Tong, sitting back and letting a search complete itself in his files. "What terrible luck! Or was it a glitch?"

Like all Chiffewarians, Tong was quite hairless—a chihuahua, in the slang of Valparaíso. To minimize his outlandishness here, where baldness was very uncommon, he wore a hat; but since the Akans seldom wore hats, he looked perhaps more alien with it than without it. He was a gentle-mannered man, informal, straightforward, putting Sutty as much at her ease as she was capable of being; yet he was so uninvasive as to be, finally, aloof. Himself uninvadable, he offered no intimacy. She was grateful that he accepted her distance. Up to now, he had kept his. But she felt his question as disingenuous. He knew, surely, that the loss of the transmission had been no accident. Why should she have to explain it? She had made it clear that she was traveling without luggage, just as Observers and Mobiles who'd been in space for centuries did. She was not answerable for the place she had left sixty light-years behind her. She was not responsible for Terra and its holy terrorism.

But the silence went on, and she said at last, "The Beijing ansible was sabotaged."

"Sabotaged?"

She nodded.

"By the Unists?"

"Toward the end of the regime there were attacks on most of the Ekumenical installations and the treaty areas. The Pales."

"Were many of them destroyed?"

He was trying to draw her out. To get her to talk about it. Anger flooded into her, rage. Her throat felt tight. She said nothing, because she was unable to say anything.

A considerable pause.

"Nothing but the language got through, then," Tong said.

"Almost nothing."

"Terrible luck!" he repeated energetically. "That the First Observers were Terran, so they sent their report to Terra instead of Hain—not unnaturally, but still, bad luck. And even worse, maybe, that ansible transmissions sent *from* Terra all got through. All the technical information the Akans asked for and Terra sent, without any question or restriction. . . . Why, why would the First Observers have agreed to such a massive cultural intervention?"

"Maybe they didn't. Maybe the Unists sent it."

"Why would the Unists start Aka marching to the stars?"

She shrugged. "Proselytising."

"You mean, persuading others to believe what they

believed? Was industrial technological progress incorporated as an element of the Unist religion?"

She kept herself from shrugging.

"So during that period when the Unists refused ansible contact with the Stabiles on Hain, they were . . . *converting* the Akans? Sutty, do you think they may have sent, what do you call them, missionaries, here?"

"I don't know."

He was not probing her, not trapping her. Eagerly pursuing his own thoughts, he was only trying to get her, a Terran, to explain to him what the Terrans had done and why. But she would not and could not explain or speak for the Unists.

Picking up her refusal to speculate, he said, "Yes, yes, I'm sorry. Of course you were scarcely in the confidence of the Unist leaders! But I've just had an idea, you see— If they did send missionaries, and if they transgressed Akan codes in some way, you see?—that might explain the Limit Law." He meant the abrupt announcement, made fifty years ago and enforced ever since, that only four offworlders would be allowed on Aka at a time, and only in the cities. "And it could explain the banning of religion a few years later!" He was carried away by his theory. He beamed, and then asked her almost pleadingly, "You never heard of a second group sent here from Terra?"

"No."

He sighed, sat back. After a minute he dismissed his speculations with a little flip of his hand. "We've been here seventy years," he said, "and all we know is the vocabulary."

She relaxed. They were off Terra, back on Aka. She was
safe. She spoke carefully, but with the fluency of relief. "In my
last year in training, some facsimile artifacts were reconstituted
from the damaged records. Pictures, a few fragments of books.
But not enough to extrapolate any major cultural elements
from. And since the Corporation State was in place when I
arrived, I don't know anything about what it replaced. I don't
even know when religion was outlawed here. About forty years
ago?" She heard her voice: placating, false, forced. Wrong.

Tong nodded. "Thirty years after the first contact with
the Ekumen. The Corporation put out the first decree declar-
ing 'religious practice and teaching' unlawful. Within a few
years they were announcing appalling penalties. . . . But
what's odd about it, what made me think the impetus might
have come from offworld, is the word they use for religion."

"Derived from Hainish," Sutty said, nodding.

"Was there no native word? Do you know one?"

"No," she said, after conscientiously going through not
only her Dovzan vocabulary but several other Akan languages she had studied at Valparaíso. "I don't."

A great deal of the recent vocabulary of Dovzan of course
came from offworld, along with the industrial technologies;
but that they should borrow a word for a native institution in
order to outlaw it? Odd indeed. And she should have noticed
it. She would have noticed it, if she had not tuned out the
word, the thing, the subject, whenever it came up. Wrong.
Wrong.

Tong had become a bit distracted; the item he had been searching for had turned up at last, and he set his noter to retrieve and decode. This took some time. "Akan microfiling leaves something to be desired," he said, poking a final key.

"'Everything breaks down on schedule,'" Sutty said. "That's the only Akan joke I know. The trouble with it is, it's true."

"But consider what they've accomplished in seventy years!" The Envoy sat back, warmly discursive, his hat slightly askew. "Rightly or wrongly, they were given the blueprint for a G86." G86 was Hainish historians' shorthand jargon for a society in fast-forward industrial technological mode. "And they devoured that information in one gulp. Remade their culture, established the Corporate worldstate, got a spaceship off to Hain—all in a single human lifetime! Amazing people, really. Amazing unity of discipline!"

Sutty nodded dutifully.

"But there must have been resistance along the way. This antireligious obsession. . . . Even if we triggered it along with the technological expansion. . . ."

It was decent of him, Sutty thought, to keep saying "we," as if the Ekumen had been responsible for Terra's intervention in Aka. That was the underlying Hainish element in Ekumenical thinking: *Take responsibility*.

The Envoy was pursuing his thought. "The mechanisms of control are so pervasive and effective, they must have been set up in response to something powerful, don't you think? If resistance to the Corporate State centered in a religion—a well-established, widespread religion—that would explain the Corporation's suppression of religious practices. And the attempt to set up national theism as a replacement. God as Reason, the Hammer of Pure Science, all that. In the name of which to destroy the temples, ban the preachings. What do you think?"

"I think it understandable," Sutty said.

It was perhaps not the response he had expected. They were silent for a minute.

"The old writing, the ideograms," Tong said, "you can read them fluently?"

"It was all there was to learn when I was in training. It was the only writing on Aka, seventy years ago."

"Of course," he said, with the disarming Chiffewarian gesture that signified *Please forgive the idiot.* "Coming from only twelve years' distance, you see, I learned only the modern script."

"Sometimes I've wondered if I'm the only person on Aka who can read the ideograms. A foreigner, an offworlder. Surely not."

"Surely not. Although the Dovzans are a systematic people. So systematic that when they banned the old script, they also systematically destroyed whatever was written in it—poems, plays, history, philosophy. Everything, you think?"

She remembered the increasing bewilderment of her

early weeks in Dovza City: her incredulity at the scant and vapid contents of what they called libraries, the blank wall that met all her attempts at research, when she had still believed there had to be some remnants, somewhere, of the literature of an entire world.

"If they find any books or texts, even now, they destroy them," she said. "One of the principal bureaus of the Ministry of Poetry is the Office of Book Location. They find books, confiscate them, and send them to be pulped for building material. Insulating material. The old books are referred to as pulpables. A woman there told me that she was going to be sent to another bureau because there were no more pulpables in Dovza. It was clean, she said. Cleansed."

She heard her voice getting edgy. She looked away, tried to ease the tension in her shoulders.

Tong Ov remained calm. "An entire history lost, wiped out, as if by a terrible disaster," he said. "Extraordinary!"

"Not that unusual," she said, very edgily— Wrong. She rearranged her shoulders again, breathed in once and out once, and spoke with conscious quietness. "The few Akan poems and drawings that were reconstructed at the Terran Ansible Center would be illegal here. I had copies with me in my noter. I erased them."

"Yes. Yes, quite right. We can't introduce anything that they don't want to have lying about."

"I hated to do it. I felt I was colluding."

"The margin between collusion and respect can be narrow," Tong said. "Unfortunately, we exist in that margin, here."

For a moment she felt a dark gravity in him. He was looking away, looking far away. Then he was back with her, genial and serene.

"But then," he said, "there are a good many scraps of the old calligraphy painted up here and there around the city, aren't there? No doubt it's considered harmless since no one now can read it. . . . And things tend to survive in out-of-the-way places. I was down in the river district one evening—it's quite disreputable, I shouldn't have been there, but now and then one can wander about in a city this size without one's hosts knowing it. At least I pretend they don't. At any rate, I heard some unusual music. Wooden instruments. Illegal intervals."

She looked her question.

"Composers are required by the Corporation State to use what I know as the Terran octave."

Sutty looked stupid.

Tong sang an octave.

Sutty tried to look intelligent.

"They call it the Scientific Scale of Intervals, here," Tong said. And still seeing no great sign of understanding, he asked, smiling, "Does Akan music sound rather more familiar to you than you had expected?"

"I hadn't thought about it—I don't know. I can't carry a tune. I don't know what keys are."

Tong's smile grew broad. "To my ear Akan music sounds

as if none of them knew what a key is. Well, what I heard down in the river district wasn't like the music on the loud-speakers at all. Different intervals. Very subtle harmonies. 'Drug music,' the people there called it. I gathered that drug music is played by faith healers, witch doctors. So one way and another I managed eventually to arrange a chat with one of these doctors. He said, 'We know some of the old songs and medicines. We don't know the stories. We can't tell them. The people who told the stories are gone.' I pressed him a little, and he said, 'Maybe some of them are still up the river there. In the mountains.'" Tong Ov smiled again, but wistfully. "I longed for more, but of course my presence there put him at risk." He made rather a long pause. "One has this sense, sometimes, that . . ."

"That it's all our fault."

After a moment he said, "Yes. It is. But since we're here, we have to try to keep our presence light."

Chiffewarians took responsibility, but did not cultivate guilt the way Terrans did. She knew she had misinterpreted him. She knew he was surprised by what she had said. But she could not keep anything light. She said nothing.

"What do you think the witch doctor meant, about sto-ries and the people who told them?"

She tried to get her mind around the question but couldn't. She could not follow him any further. She knew what the saying meant: to come to the end of your tether. Her tether choked her, tight around her throat.

She said, "I thought you sent for me to tell me you were transferring me."

"Off the planet? No! No, no," Tong said, with surprise and a quiet kindness.

"I shouldn't have been sent here."

"Why do you say that?"

"I trained as a linguist and in literature. Aka has one language left and no literature. I wanted to be a historian. How can I, on a world that's destroyed its history?"

"It's not easy," Tong said feelingly. He got up to check the file recorder. He said, "Please tell me, Sutty, is the institutionalised homophobia very difficult for you?"

"I grew up with it."

"Under the Unists."

"Not only the Unists."

"I see," Tong said. Still standing, he spoke carefully, looking at her; she looked down. "I know that you lived through a great religious upheaval. And I think of Terra as a world whose history has been shaped by religions. So I see you as the best fitted of us to investigate the vestiges, if they exist, of this world's religion. Ki Ala has no experience of religion, you see, and Garru has no detachment from it." He stopped again. She made no response. "Your experience," he said, "may have been of a kind that would make detachment difficult for you. To have lived all your life under theocratic repression, and the turmoil and violence of the last years of Unism. . . ."

She had to speak. She said coldly, "I believe my training will allow me to observe another culture without excessive prejudice."

"Your training and your own temperament: yes. I believe so too. But the pressures of an aggressive theocracy, the great weight of it all through your life, may well have left you a residue of distrust, of resistance. If I'm asking you—again!—to observe something you detest, please tell me that."

After a few seconds which seemed long to her she said, "I really am no good at all with music."

"I think the music is a small element of something very large," said Tong, doe-eyed, implacable.

"I see no problem, then," she said. She felt cold, false, defeated. Her throat ached.

Tong waited a little for her to say more, and then accepted her word. He picked up the microcrystal record and gave it to her. She took it automatically.

"Read this and listen to the music here in the library, please, and then erase it," he said. "Erasure is an art we must learn from the Akans. Seriously! I mean it. The Hainish want to hang on to everything. The Akans want to throw everything away. Maybe there's a middle way? At any rate, we have our first chance to get into an area where maybe history wasn't erased so thoroughly."

"I don't know if I'll know what I'm seeing when I see it. Ki Ala's been here ten years. You've had experience on four other worlds." She had told him there was no problem. She had said she could do what he asked. Now she heard herself still trying to whine her way out of it. Wrong. Shameful.

"I've never lived through a great social revolution," Tong said. "Nor has Ki Ala. We're children of peace, Sutty. I need a child of conflict. Anyhow, Ki Ala is illiterate. I am illiterate. You can read."

"Dead languages in a banned script."

Tong looked at her again for a minute in silence, with an intellectual, impersonal, real tenderness. "I believe you tend to undervalue your capacities, Sutty," he said. "The Stabiles chose you to be one of the four representatives of the Ekumen on Aka. I need you to accept the fact that your experience and your knowledge are essential to me, to our work here. Please consider that."

He waited until she said, "I will."

"Before you go up to the mountains, if you do, I also want you to consider the risks. Or rather to consider the fact that we don't know what the risks may be. The Akans seem not to be a violent people; but that's hard to judge from our insulated position. I don't know why they've suddenly given us this permission. Surely they have some reason or motive, but we can find what it is only by taking advantage of it." He paused, his eyes still on her. "There's no mention of your being accompanied, of having guides, watchdogs. You may be quite on your own. You may not. We don't know. None of us knows what life is like outside the cities. Every difference or sameness, everything you see, everything you read, everything you record, will be important. I know already that you're a sensitive and impartial observer. And if there's any history left on Aka, you're the member of my crew here best suited to find it. To go look for these 'stories,' or the people who know them. So, please, listen to these songs, and then go home and think about it, and tell me your decision tomorrow. *O.K.?*"

He said the old Terran phrase stiffly, with some pride in the accomplishment. Sutty tried to smile. "O.K.," she said.

TWO

ON THE WAY home, in the monorail, she suddenly broke
into tears. Nobody noticed. Crowded in the car, people tired
from work and dulled by the long rocking ride all sat watching the holopro above the aisle: children doing gymnastics,
hundreds of tiny children in red uniforms kicking and jumping in unison to shrill cheery music in the air.

On the long climb up the stairs to her apartment she
wept again. There was no reason to cry. There had to be a
reason. She must be sick. The misery she felt was fear, a
wretched panic of fear. Dread. Terror. It was crazy to send her
off on her own. Tong was crazy to think of it. She could never
handle it. She sat down at her workdesk to send him a formal

request for return to Terra. The Hainish words would not come. They were all wrong.

Her head ached. She got up to find something to eat. There was nothing in her foodstorage, nothing at all. When had she eaten last? Not at midday. Not in the morning. Not last night.

"What's wrong with me?" she said to the air. No wonder her stomach hurt. No wonder she had fits of weeping and panic. She had never in her life forgotten to eat. Even in that time, the time after, when she went back to Chile, even then she had cooked food and eaten it, forcing food salty with tears down her throat day after day after day.

"I won't do this," she said. She didn't know what she meant. She refused to go on crying.

She walked back down the stairs, flashed her ZIL at the exit, walked ten blocks to the nearest Corp-Star foodshop, flashed her ZIL at the entrance. All the foods were packaged, processed, frozen, convenient; nothing fresh, nothing to cook. The sight of the wrapped rows made her tears break out again. Furious and humiliated, she bought a hot stuffed roll at the Eat Quick counter. The man serving was too busy to look at her face.

She stood outside the shop on the street, turned away from people passing by, and crammed the food into her mouth, salty with tears, forced herself to swallow, just like back then, back there. Back then she had known she had to live. It was her job. To live life after joy. Leave love and death behind her. Go on. Go alone and work. And now she was going to ask to get sent back to Earth? Back to death?

She chewed and swallowed. Music and slogans blared in broken bursts from passing vehicles. The light at a crossing four blocks away had failed, and robocab horns outblared the music. People on foot, the producer-consumers of the Corporation State, in uniforms of rust, tan, blue, green, or in Corporation-made standard trousers, tunics, jackets, all wearing canvas StarMarch shoes, came crowding past, coming up from the underground garages, hurrying toward one apartment house or another.

Sutty chewed and swallowed the last tough, sweet-salt lump of food. She would not go back. She would go on. Go alone and work. She went back to her apartment house, flashed her ZIL at the entrance, and climbed the eight flights of stairs. She had been given a big, flashy, top-floor apartment because it was considered suitable for an honored guest of the Corporation State. The elevator had not been working for a month.

She nearly missed the boat. The robocab got lost trying to find the river. It took her to the Aquarium, then to the Bureau of Water Resources and Processing, then to the Aquarium again. She had to override it and reprogram it three times. As she scurried across the wharf, the crew of

Ereha River Ferry Eight was just pulling in the gangway. She shouted, they shoved the gangway back down, she scrambled aboard. She tossed her bags into her tiny cabin and came out on deck to watch the city go by.

It showed a dingier, quieter side down here on the water, far under the canyon walls of the blocks and towers of business and government. Beneath huge concrete embankments were wooden docks and warehouses black with age, a water-beetle come-and-go of little boats on errands that were no doubt beneath the notice of the Ministry of Commerce, and houseboat communities wreathed in flowering vines, flapping laundry, and the stink of sewage.

A stream ran through a concrete ditch between high dark walls to join the great river. Above it a fisherman leaned on the rail of a humpback bridge: a silhouette, simple, immobile, timeless—the image of a drawing in one of the Akan books they had partially salvaged from the lost transmission.

How reverently she had handled those few pages of images, lines of poems, fragments of prose, how she had pored over them, back in Valparaíso, trying to feel from them what these people of another world were like, longing to know them. It had been hard to erase the copies from her noter, here, and no matter what Tong said, she still felt it as a wrong, a capitulation to the enemy. She had studied the copies in her noter one last time, lovingly, painfully, trying to hold on to them before she deleted them. *And there are no footprints in the dust behind us. . . .* She had shut her eyes as she deleted that poem. Doing so, she felt that she was erasing all her yearning hope that when she came to Aka she'd learn what it was about.

But she remembered the four lines of the poem, and the hope and yearning were still there.

The quiet engines of Ferry Eight drummed softly. Hour by hour the embankments grew lower, older, more often broken by stairs and landings. At last they sank away altogether into mud and reeds and shrubby banks, and the Ereha spread itself out wider and wider and amazingly wider across a flatness of green and yellow-green fields.

For five days the boat, moving steadily eastward on that steady breadth of water through mild sunshine and mild starry darkness, was the tallest thing in sight. Now and then it came to a riverside city where it would tie up at an old dock dwarfed under high new office and apartment towers and take on supplies and passengers.

Sutty found it amazingly easy to talk to people on the boat. In Dovza City everything had conspired to keep her reserved and silent. Though the four offworlders were given apartments and a certain freedom of movement, the Corporation scheduled their lives very closely with appointments, programming and supervising their work and amusements. Not that they were the only ones so controlled: Aka's abrupt and tremendous technological advance was sustained by rigid discipline universally enforced and self-enforced. It seemed that everybody in the city worked hard, worked long hours, slept short hours, ate in haste. Every hour was scheduled. Everybody she'd been in touch with in the Ministries of Poetry and of Information knew exactly what they wanted her to do and how she should do it, and as soon as she started doing as they directed, they hurried off about their business, leaving her to hers.

Though the technologies and achievements of the Ekumenical worlds were held as the shining model for everything on Aka, the four visitors from the Ekumen were kept, as Tong said, in a fish tank. From time to time they were put on display to the public and in the neareals, smiling figures sitting at a Corporation banquet or somewhere near the chief of a bureau giving a speech; but they were not asked to speak. Only to smile. Possibly the ministers did not trust them to say exactly what they ought to say. Possibly the ministers found them rather flat, dull examples of the superior civilisations Aka was striving so hard to emulate. Most civilisations, perhaps, look shinier in general terms and from several light-years away.

Though Sutty had met many Akans and disliked few of them, after a half year on the planet she had scarcely had anything deserving the name of a conversation with any one of them. She had seen nothing of Akan private life except the stiff dinner parties of upper-level bureaucrats and Corporation officials. No personal friendship had ever come even remotely into view. No doubt the people she met had been advised not to talk with her more than necessary, so that the

Corporation could remain in full control of the information she received. But even with people she saw constantly, intimacy did not grow. She did not feel this distance as prejudice, xenophobia; the Akans were remarkably unconcerned about foreignness as such. It was that they were all so busy, and all bureaucrats. Conversation went by program. At the banquets people talked business, sports, and technology. Waiting in lines or at the laundry, they talked sports and the latest neareals. They avoided the personal and, in public, repeated the Corporation line on all matters of policy and opinion, to the point of contradicting her when her description of her world didn't tally with what they had been taught about wonderful, advanced, resourceful Terra.

But on the riverboat, people talked. They talked personally, intimately, and exhaustively. They leaned on the railing talking, sat around on the deck talking, stayed at the dinner table with a glass of wine talking.

A word or smile from her was enough to include her in their talk. And she realised, slowly, because it took her by surprise, that they didn't know she was an alien.

They all knew there were Observers from the Ekumen on Aka; they'd seen them on the neareals, four infinitely remote, meaningless figures among the ministers and executives, stuffed aliens among the stuffed shirts; but they had no expectation of meeting one among ordinary people.

She had expected not only to be recognised but to be set apart and kept at a remove wherever she traveled. But no guides had been offered and no supervisors were apparent. It seemed that the Corporation had decided to let her be genuinely on her own. She had been on her own in the city, but in the fish tank, a bubble of isolation. The bubble had popped. She was outside.

It was a little frightening when she thought about it, but she didn't think much about it, because it was such a pleasure. She was accepted—one of the travelers, one of the crowd. She didn't have to explain, didn't have to evade explanation, because they didn't ask. She spoke Dovzan with no more accent, indeed less, than many Akans from regions other than Dovza. People assumed from her physical type— short, slight, dark-skinned—that she came from the east of the continent. "You're from the east, aren't you?" they said. "My cousin Muniti married a man from Turu," and then they went on talking about themselves.

She heard about them, their cousins, their families, their jobs, their opinions, their houses, their hernias. People with pets traveled by riverboat, she discovered, petting a woman's furry and affable kittypup. People who disliked or feared flying took the boat, as a chatty old gentleman told her in vast detail. People not in a hurry went by boat and told each other their stories. Sutty got told even more stories than most, because she listened without interrupting, except to say, Really? What happened then? and How wonderful! or How terrible! She listened with greed, tireless. These dull and fragmentary relations of ordinary lives could not bore her. Everything she had missed in Dovza City, everything the official literature, the heroic propaganda left out, they told. If she had to choose between heroes and hernias, it was no contest.

As they got farther upstream, deeper inland, passengers of a different kind began to come aboard. Country people used the riverboat as the simplest and cheapest way to get from one town to another—walk onto the boat here and get off it there. The towns were smaller now, without tall buildings. By the seventh day, passengers were boarding not with pets and luggage but with fowls in baskets, goats on leashes.

They weren't exactly goats, or deer or cows or any other earthly thing; they were eberdin; but they blatted, and had silky hair, and in Sutty's mental ecology they occupied the goat niche. They were raised for milk, meat, and the silky hair. In the old days, according to a bright-colored page of a picture book that had survived the lost transmission, eberdin had pulled carts and even carried riders. She remembered the blue-and-red banners on the cart, and the inscription under the picture: SETTING OFF FOR THE GOLDEN MOUNTAIN. She wondered if it had been a fantasy for children, or a larger breed of eberdin. Nobody could ride these; they were only about knee-high. By the eighth day they were coming aboard in flocks. The aft deck was knee-deep in eberdin.

The city folk with pets and the aerophobes had all disembarked early that morning at Eltli, a big town that ran a railway line up into the South Headwaters Range resort country.

Near Eltli the Ereha went through three locks, one very deep. Above them it was a different river—wilder, narrower, faster, its water not cloudy blue-brown but airy blue-green.

Long conversations also ended at Eltli. The country folk now on the boat were not unfriendly but were shy of strangers, talking mostly to their own acquaintances, in dialect. Sutty welcomed her recovered solitude, which left her eyes to see.

Off to the left as the stream bent north, mountain peaks spired up one after another, black rock, white glaciers. Ahead of the boat, upstream, no peaks were visible, nothing dramatic; the land just went slowly up, and up, and up. And Ferry Eight, now full of blatting and squawking and the quiet, intermittent voices of the country people, and smelling of manure, fried bread, fish, and sweet melons, moved slowly, her silent engines working hard against the drastic current, between wide rocky shores and treeless plains of thin, pale, plumy grass. Curtains of rain swept across the land, dropping from vast, quick clouds, and trailed off leaving sunlight, diamond air, the fragrance of the soil. Night was silent, cold, starlit. Sutty stayed up late and waked early. She came out on deck. The east was brightening. Over the shadowy western plains, dawn lit the far peaks one by one like matches.

The boat stopped where no town or village was, no sign of habitation. A woman in fleece tunic and felt hat crowded her flock onto the gangplank, and they ran ashore, she running with them, shouting curses at them and raucous goodbyes to friends aboard. From the aft rail Sutty watched the flock for miles, a shrinking pale blot on the grey-gold plain. All that ninth day passed in a trance of light. The boat moved slowly. The river, now clear as the wind, rushed by so silently that the boat seemed to float above it, between two airs. All around them were levels of rock and pale grass, pale distances. The mountains were lost, hidden by the vast swell of rising land. Land, and sky, and the river crossing from one to the other.

This is a longer journey, Sutty thought, standing again at the rail that evening, than my journey from Earth to Aka.

And she thought of Tong Ov, who might have made this journey himself and had given it to her to make, and wondered how to thank him. By seeing, by describing, by recording, yes. But she could not record her happiness. The word itself destroyed it.

She thought: Pao should be here. By me. She would have been here. We would have been happy.

The air darkened, the water held the light.

One other person was on deck. He was the only other passenger who had been on the boat all the way from the capital, a silent, fortyish man, a Corporation official in blue and tan. Uniforms were ubiquitous on Aka. Schoolchildren wore scarlet shorts and tunics: masses and lines and little hopping dots of brilliant red all over the streets of the cities, a startling, cheerful sight. College students wore green and rust. Blue and tan was the Sociocultural Bureau, which included the

Central Ministry of Poetry and Art and the World Ministry of
Information. Sutty was very familiar with blue and tan. Poets
wore blue and tan—official poets, at any rate—and produc-
ers of tapes and neareals, and librarians, and bureaucrats in
branches of the bureau with which Sutty was less familiar,
such as Ethical Purity. The insignia on this man's jacket
identified him as a Monitor, fairly high in the hierarchy.
When she was first aboard, expecting some kind of official
presence or supervision, some watchdog watching her excur-
sion, Sutty had waited for him to show some attention to her
or evidence of keeping an eye on her. She saw nothing of the
kind. If he knew who she was, nothing in his demeanor
showed it. He had been entirely silent and aloof, ate at the
captain's table at meals, communicated only with his noter,
and avoided the groups of talkers that she always joined.

Now he came to stand at the rail not far from her. She
nodded and ignored him, which was what he had always
appeared to want.

But he spoke, breaking the intense silence of the vast
dusk landscape, where only the water murmured its resistance quietly and fiercely to the boat's prow and sides. "A
dreary country," the Monitor said.

His voice roused a young eberdin tied to a stanchion
nearby. It bleated softly, Ma-ma! and shook its head.

"Barren," the man said. "Backward. Are you interested in
lovers' eyes?"

Ma-ma! said the little eberdin.

"Excuse me?" said Sutty.

"Lovers' eyes. Gems, jewels."

"Why are they called that?"

"Primitive fancy. Imagined resemblance." The man's glance crossed hers for a moment. In so far as she had thought anything about him at all, she had thought him stiff and dull, a little egocrat. The cold keenness of his look surprised her.

"They're found along stream banks, in the high country. Only there," he said, pointing upstream, "and only on this planet. I take it some other interest brought you here."

He did know who she was, then. And from his manner, he wished her to know that he disapproved of her being on the loose, on her own.

"In the short time I've been on Aka, I've seen only Dovza City. I received permission to do some sightseeing."

"To go upriver," the man said with a tight pseudo-smile. He waited for more. She felt a pressure from him, an expectancy, as if he considered her accountable to him. She resisted.

He gazed at the purplish plains fading into night and then down at the water that seemed still to hold some transparency of light within it. He said, "Dovza is a land of beautiful scenery. Rich farmlands, prosperous industries, delightful resorts in the South Headwaters Range. Having seen nothing of that, why did you choose to visit this desert?"

"I come from a desert," Sutty said.

That shut him up for a bit.

"We know that Terra is a rich, progressive world." His voice was dark with disapproval.

"Some of my world is fertile. Much of it is still barren. We have misused it badly. . . . It's a whole world, Monitor. With room enough for a lot of variety. Just as here."

She heard the note of challenge in her voice.

"Yet you prefer barren places and backward methods of travel?"

This was not the exaggerated respect shown her by people in Dovza City, who had treated her as a fragile exotic that must be sheltered from reality. This was suspicion, distrust. He was telling her that aliens should not be allowed to wander about alone. The first xenophobia she'd met on Aka.

"I like boats," she said, with care, pleasantly. "And I find this country beautiful. Austere but beautiful. Don't you?"

"No," he said, an order. No disagreement allowed. The corporate, official voice.

"So what brings you up the river? Are you looking for lovers' eyes?" She spoke lightly, even a bit flirtily, allowing him to change tone and get out of the challenge-response mode if he wanted to.

He didn't. "Business," he said. *Vizdiat*, the ultimate Akan justification, the inarguable aim, the bottom line. "There are pockets of cultural fossilisation and recalcitrant reactionary activity in this area. I hope you have no intention of traveling out of town into the high country. Where education has not yet reached, the natives are brutal and dangerous. In so far as I have jurisdiction in this area, I must ask you to remain in touch with my office at all times, to report any evidence of illegal practices, and to inform us if you plan to travel."

"I appreciate your concern and shall endeavor to comply with your request," Sutty said, straight out of *Advanced Exercises in Dovzan Usage and Locutions for Barbarians.*

The Monitor nodded once, his eyes on the slowly passing, slowly darkening shore. When she looked again where he had stood he was gone.

THREE

THE WONDERFUL VOYAGE of a ship climbing a river through a desert ended on the tenth day at Okzat-Ozkat. On the map the town had been a dot at the edge of an endless tangle of contour lines, the High Headwaters Range. In the late evening it was a blur of whitish walls in the clear, cold darkness, dim horizontal windows set high, smells of dust and dung and rotten fruit and a dry sweetness of mountain air, a singsong of voices, the clatter of shod feet on stone. Scarcely any wheeled traffic. A gleam of rusty light shone on some kind of high, pale, distant wall, faintly visible above ornate roofs, against the last greenish clarity of the western sky.

Corporation announcements and music blared across

the wharfs. That noise after ten days of quiet voices and river
silence drove Sutty straight away.

No tour guide was waiting for her. Nobody followed her.
Nobody asked her to show her ZIL.

Still in the passive trance of the journey, curious, nervous, alert, she wandered through the streets near the river till
her shoulder bag began to drag her down and she felt the
knife edge of the wind. In a dark, small street that ran uphill
she stopped at a doorway. The house door was open, and a
woman sat in a chair in the yellow light from within the
house as if enjoying a balmy summer evening.

"Can you tell me where I might find an inn?"

"Here," the woman said. She was crippled, Sutty saw
now, with legs like sticks. "Ki!" she called.

A boy of fifteen or so appeared. Wordlessly he invited
Sutty into the house. He showed her to a high-ceilinged, big,
dark room on the ground floor, furnished with a rug. It was a
magnificent rug, crimson eberdin wool with severe, complex,
concentric patterns in black and white. The only other thing
in the room was the light fixture, a peculiar, squarish bulb,
quite dim, fixed between two high-set, horizontal windows.
Its cord came snaking in one of the windows.

"Is there a bed?"

The boy gestured shyly to a curtain in the shadows of the
far corner.

"Bath?"

He ducked his head toward a door. Sutty went and

opened it. Three tiled steps went down to a little tiled room in which were various strange but interpretable devices of wood, metal, and ceramic, shining in the warm glow of an electric heater.

"It looks very nice," she said. "How much is it?"

"Eleven haha," the boy murmured.

"The night?"

"For a week." The Akan week was ten days.

"Oh, that's very nice," Sutty said. "Thank you."

Wrong. She should not have thanked him. Thanks were "servile address." Honorifics and meaningless ritual phrases of greeting, leave-taking, permission-asking, and false gratitude, please, thank you, you're welcome, goodbye, fossil relics of primitive hypocrisy—all were stumbling blocks to truthfulness between producer-consumers. She had learned that lesson, in those terms, almost as soon as she arrived. She had trained herself quite out of any such bad habits acquired on Earth. What had made the uncouth thanks jump now from her mouth?

The boy only murmured something which she had to ask him to repeat: an offer of dinner. She accepted without thanks.

In half an hour he brought a low table into her room, set with a figured cloth and dishes of dark-red porcelain. She had found cushions and a fat bedroll behind the curtain; had hung up her clothes on the bar and pegs also behind the curtain; had set her books and notebooks on the polished floor under the single light; and now sat on the carpet doing nothing. She liked the extraordinary sense of room in this room—space, height, stillness.

The boy served her a dinner of roast poultry, roast vegetables, a white grain that tasted like corn, and lukewarm, aromatic tea. She sat on the silky rug and ate it all. The boy looked in silently a couple of times to see if she needed anything.

"'Tell me the name of this cereal, please." No. Wrong. "But first, tell me your name."

"Akidan," he whispered. "That's tuzi."

"It's very good. I never ate it before. Does it grow here?"

Akidan nodded. He had a strong, sweet face, still childish, but the man visible. "It's good for the wood," he murmured.

Sutty nodded sagely. "And delicious."

"Thank you, yoz." Yoz: a term defined by the Corporation as servile address and banned for the last fifty years at least. It meant, more or less, fellow person. Sutty had never heard the word spoken except on the tapes from which she had learned Akan languages back on Earth. And 'good for the wood,' was that an evil fossil of some kind too? She might find out tomorrow. Tonight she'd have a bath, unroll her bed, and sleep in the dark, blessed silence of this high place.

———

A gentle knock, presumably by Akidan, guided her to breakfast waiting on the tray-table outside her door. There was a big piece of cut and seeded fruit, bits of something yellow and pungent in a saucer, a crumbly greyish cake, and a handleless mug of lukewarm tea, this time faintly bitter, with a taste she disliked at first but found increasingly satisfying. The fruit and bread were fresh and delicate. She left the yellow pickled bits. When the boy came to remove the tray, she asked the name of everything, for this food was entirely different from anything she had eaten in the capital, and it had been presented with significant care. The pickled thing was abid, Akidan said. "It's for the early morning," he said, "to help the sweet fruit."

"So I should eat it?"

He smiled, embarrassed. "It helps to balance."

"I see. I'll eat it, then." She ate it. Akidan seemed pleased. "I come from very far away, Akidan," she said.

"Dovza City."

"Farther. Another world. Terra of the Ekumen."

"Ah."

"So I'm ignorant about how to live here. I'd like to ask you lots of questions. Is that all right?"

He gave a little shrug-nod, very adolescent. Shy as he was, he was self-possessed. Whatever it meant to him, he accepted with aplomb the fact that an Observer of the Ekumen, an alien whom he could have expected to see only as an electronic image sent from the capital, was living in his house. Not a trace of the xenophobia she had diagnosed in the disagreeable man on the boat.

Akidan's aunt, the crippled woman, who looked as if she was in constant low-level pain, spoke little and did not smile, but had the same tranquil, acceptant manner. Sutty arranged with her to stay two weeks, possibly longer. She had wondered if she was the only guest at the inn; now, finding her way about the house, she saw there was only one guest room.

In the city, at every hotel and apartment house, restaurant, shop, store, office, or bureau, every entrance and exit ran an automatic check of your personal ID chip, the all-important ZIL, the warranty of your existence as a producer-consumer entered in the data banks of the Corporation. Her ZIL had been issued her during the lengthy formalities of entrance at the spaceport. Without it, she had been warned, she had no identity on Aka. She could not hire a room or a robocab, buy food at a market or in a restaurant, or enter any public building without setting off an alarm. Most Akans had their chip embedded in the left wrist. She had taken the option of wearing hers in a fitted bracelet. Speaking with Akidan's aunt in the little front office, she found herself looking around for the ZIL scanner, holding her left arm ready to make the universal gesture. But the woman pivoted her chair to a massive desk with dozens of small drawers in it. After quite a few tranquil mistakes and pauses to ponder, she found the drawer she wanted and extracted a dusty booklet of forms, one of which she tore off. She pivoted the chair back round and handed the form to Sutty to fill out by hand. It was so old that the paper was crumbly, but it did have a space for the ZIL code.

"Please, yoz, tell me how to address you," Sutty said, another sentence from the *Advanced Exercises*.

"My name is Iziezi. Please tell me how to address you, yoz and deyberienduin."

Welcome-my-roof-under. A nice word. "My name is Sutty, yoz and kind innkeeper." Invented for the occasion, but it seemed to serve the purpose. Iziezi's thin, drawn face warmed faintly. When Sutty gave her the form back, she drew her clasped hands against her breastbone with a slight but very formal inclination of the head. A banned gesture if ever there was one. Sutty returned it.

As she left, Iziezi was putting the form book and the form Sutty had filled out into a desk drawer, not the same one. It looked as if the Corporation State was not going to know, for a few hours anyhow, exactly where individual /EX/HH 440 T 386733849 H 4/4939 was staying.

I've escaped the net, Sutty thought, and walked out into the sunshine.

Inside the house it was rather dim, all the horizontal windows being set very high up in the wall so that they showed nothing but fierce blue sky. Coming outdoors, she was dazzled. White house walls, glittering roof tiles, steep streets of dark slate flashing back the light. Above the roofs westward, as she began to be able to see again, she saw the highest of the white walls—immensely high—a wrinkled curtain of light halfway up the sky. She stood blinking, staring. Was it a cloud? A volcanic eruption? The Northern Lights in daytime?

"Mother," said a small, toothless, dirt-colored man with a three-wheeled barrow, grinning at her from the street.

Sutty blinked at him.

"Ereha's mother," he said, and gestured at the wall of light. "Silong. Eh?"

Mount Silong. On the map, the highest point of the Headwaters Range and of the Great Continent of Aka. Yes. As they came up the river, the rise of the land had kept it hidden. Here you could see perhaps the upper half of it, a serrated radiance above which floated, still more remote, immense, ethereal, a horned peak half dissolved in golden light. From the summit streamed the thin snow-banners of eternal wind.

As she and the barrow man stood gazing, others stopped to help them gaze. That was the impression Sutty got. They all knew what Silong looked like and therefore could help her see it. They said its name and called it Mother, pointing to the glitter of the river down at the foot of the street. One of them said, "You might go to Silong, yoz?"

They were small, thin people, with the padded cheeks and narrow eyes of hill dwellers, bad teeth, patched clothes, thin, fine hands and feet coarsened by cold and injury. They were about the same color of brown she was.

"Go there?" She looked at them all smiling and could not help smiling. "Why?"

"On Silong you live forever," said a gnarly woman with a backpack full of what looked like pumice rock.

"Caves," said a man with a yellowish, scarred face. "Caves full of being."

"Good sex!" said the barrow man, and everybody laughed. "Sex for three hundred years!"

"It's too high," Sutty said, "how could anybody go there?"

They all grinned and said, "Fly!"

"Could a plane land on that?"

Cackles, headshakes. The gnarly woman said, "Nowhere," the yellow man said, "No planes," and the barrow man said, "After three-hundred-year sex, anybody can fly!" And then as they were all laughing they stopped, they wavered like shadows, they vanished, and nobody was there except the barrow man trundling his barrow halfway down the street, and Sutty staring at the Monitor.

On the ship she had not seen him as a big man, but here he loomed. His skin, his flesh, were different from that of the people here, smooth, tough, and even, like plastic. His blue-and-tan tunic and leggings were clean and smooth and like uniforms everywhere on every world, and he didn't belong in Okzat-Ozkat any more than she did. He was an alien.

"Begging is illegal," he said.

"I wasn't begging."

After a slight pause he said, "You misunderstand. Do not

encourage beggars. They are parasites on the economy. Alms-
giving is illegal."

"No one was begging."

He gave his short nod—all right then, consider yourself
warned—and turned away.

"Thank you so much for your charm and courtesy!"
Sutty said in her native language. Oh, wrong, wrong. She
had no business being sarcastic in any language, even if the
Monitor paid no attention. He was insufferable, but that did
not excuse her. If she was to obtain any information here, she
must stay in the good graces of local officialdom; if she was to
learn anything here, she must not be judgmental. The old
farfetchers' motto: *Opinion ends reception.* Maybe those
people had in fact been beggars, working her. How did she
know? She knew nothing, nothing about this place, these
people.

She set off to learn her way around Okzat-Ozkat with the
humble determination not to have any opinions about it at all.

The modern buildings—prison, district and civic prefec-
tures, agricultural, cultural, and mining agencies, teachers'
college, high school—looked like all such buildings in the
other cities she'd seen: plain, massive blocks. Here they were
only two or three stories high, but they loomed, the way the
Monitor did. The rest of the city was small, subtle, dirty, fragile. Low house walls washed red or orange, horizontal windows set high under the eaves, roofs of red or olive-green tile
with curlicues running up the angles and fantastic ceramic

animals pulling up the corners in their toothy mouths; little shops, their outer and inner walls entirely covered with writing in the old ideographs, whitewashed over but showing through with a queer subliminal legibility. Steep slate-paved streets and steps leading up to locked doors painted red and blue and whitewashed over. Work yards where men made rope or cut stone. Narrow plots between houses where old women dug and hoed and weeded and changed the flow patterns of miniature irrigation systems. A few cars down by the docks and parked by the big white buildings, but the street traffic all on foot and by barrow and handcart. And, to Sutty's delight, a caravan coming in from the country: big eberdin pulling two-wheeled carts with green-fringed tent tops, and two even bigger eberdin, the size of ponies, with bells tied in the creamy wool of their necks, each ridden by a woman in a long red coat sitting impassive in the high, horned saddle.

The caravan passed the facade of the District Prefecture, a tiny, jaunty, jingling scrap of the past creeping by under the blank gaze of the future. Inspirational music interspersed with exhortations blared from the roof of the Prefecture. Sutty followed the caravan for several blocks and watched it stop at the foot of one of the long flights of steps. People in the street also stopped, with that same amiable air of helping her watch, though they said nothing to her. People came out the high red and blue doors and down the steps to welcome the riders and carry in the luggage. A hotel? The owners' townhouse?

She climbed back up to one of the shops she had passed in the higher part of town. If she had understood the signs around the door, the shop sold lotions, unguents, smells, and fertiliser. A purchase of hand cream might give her time to read some of the inscriptions that covered every wall from floor to ceiling, all in the old, the illegal writing. On the facade of the shop the inscriptions had been whitewashed out and painted over with signs in the modern alphabet, but these had faded enough that she could make out some of the underlying words. That was where she had made out "smells and fertiliser." Probably perfumes and—what? Fertility? Fertility drugs, maybe? She went in.

She was at once engulfed in the smells—powerful, sweet, sharp, strange. A dim, pungent air. She had the curious sensation that the pictographs and ideograms that covered the walls with bold black and dark-blue shapes were moving, not jumpily like half-seen print but evenly, regularly, expanding and shrinking very gently, as if they were breathing.

The room was high, lighted by the usual high-set windows, and lined with cabinets full of little drawers. As her eyes adjusted, she saw that a thin old man stood behind a counter to her left. Behind his head two characters stood out quite clearly on the wall. She read them automatically, various of their various meanings arriving more or less at once: *eminent / peak / felt hat / look down / start up*, and *two / duality / sides / loins / join / separate*.

"Yoz and deyberienduin, may I be of use to you?"

She asked if he had an unguent or lotion for dry skin. The proprietor nodded pleasantly and began seeking among his thousand little drawers with an air of peaceful certainty of eventually finding what he wanted, like Iziezi at her desk.

This gave Sutty time to read the walls, but that distracting illusion of movement continued, and she could not make much sense of the writings. They seemed not to be advertisements as she had assumed, but recipes, or charms, or quotations. A lot about branches and roots. A character she knew as blood, but written with a different Elemental qualifier, which might make it mean lymph, or sap. Formulas like "the five from the three, the three from the five." Alchemy? Medicine, prescriptions, charms? All she knew was that these were old words, old meanings, that for the first time she was reading Aka's past. And it made no sense.

To judge by his expression, the proprietor had found a drawer he liked. He gazed into it for some while with a satisfied look before he took an unglazed clay jar out of it and put it down on the counter. Then he went back to seeking gently among the rows of unlabeled drawers until he found another one he approved of. He opened it and gazed into it and, after a while, took out a gold-paper box. With this he disappeared into an inner room. Presently he came back with the box, a small, brightly glazed pot, and a spoon. He set them all down on the counter in a row. He spooned out something from the unglazed pot into the glazed pot, wiped the spoon with a red cloth he took from under the counter, mixed two spoonfuls

of a fine, talc-like powder from the gold box into the glazed
pot, and began to stir the mixture with the same unhurried
patience. "It will make the bark quite smooth," he said softly.

"The bark," Sutty repeated.

He smiled and, setting down the spoon, smoothed one
hand over the back of the other.

"The body is like a tree?"

"Ah," he said, the way Akidan had said, "Ah." It was a
sound of assent, but qualified. It was yes but not quite yes. Or
yes but we don't use that word. Or yes but we don't need to
talk about that. Yes with a loophole.

"*In the dark cloud descending out of the sky . . . the
forked . . . the twice-forked . . . ?*" Sutty said, trying to read a
faded but magnificently written inscription high on the wall.

The proprietor slapped one hand loudly on the counter
and the other over his mouth.

Sutty jumped.

They stared at each other. The old man lowered his
hand. He seemed undisturbed, despite his startling reaction.
He was perhaps smiling. "Not aloud, yoz," he murmured.

Sutty went on staring for a moment, then shut her mouth.

"Just old decorations," the proprietor said. "Old-fashioned
wallpaper. Senseless dots and lines. Old-fashioned people live
around here. They leave these old decorations around instead
of painting walls clean and white. White and silent. Silence is
snowfall. Now, yoz and honored customer, this ointment per-
mits the skin to breathe mildly. Will you try it?"

She dipped a finger in the pot and spread the dab of pale cream on her hands. "Oh, very nice. And what a pleasant smell. What is it called?"

"The scent is the herb immimi, and the ointment is my secret, and the price is nothing."

Sutty had picked up the pot and was admiring it; it was surely an old piece, enamel on heavy glass, with an elegantly fitted cap, a little jewel. "Oh, no, no, no," she said, but the old man raised his clasped hands as Iziezi had done and bowed his head with such dignity that further protest was impossible. She repeated his gesture. Then she smiled and said, "Why?"

". . . *the twice-forked lightning-tree grows up from earth,*" he said almost inaudibly.

After a moment she looked back up at the inscription and saw that it ended with the words he had spoken. Their eyes met again. Then he melted into the dim back part of the room and she was out on the street, blinking in the glare, clutching the gift.

Walking back down the steep, complicated streets to her inn, she pondered. It seemed that first the Mobile, then the Monitor, and now the Fertiliser, or whatever he was, had promptly and painlessly co-opted her, involving her in their intentions without telling her what they were. Go find the people who know the stories and report back to me, Tong said. Avoid dissident reactionaries and report back to me, said the Monitor. As for the Fertiliser, had he bribed her to be silent or rewarded her for speaking? The latter, she thought.

But all she was certain of was that she was far too ignorant to do what she was doing without danger to herself or others.

The government of this world, to gain technological power and intellectual freedom, had outlawed the past. She did not underestimate the enmity of the Akan Corporation State toward the "old decorations" and what they meant. To this government who had declared they would be free of tradition, custom, and history, all old habits, ways, modes, manners, ideas, pieties were sources of pestilence, rotten corpses to be burned or buried. The writing that had preserved them was to be erased.

If the educational tapes and historical neareal dramas she had studied in the capital were factual, as she thought they were at least in part, within the lifetime of people now living, men and women had been crushed under the walls of temples, burned alive with books they tried to save, imprisoned for life for teaching anachronistic sedition and reactionary ideology. The tapes and dramas glorified this war against the past, relating the bombings, burnings, bulldozings in sternly heroic terms. Brave young men and women broke free from stupid parents, conniving priests, teachers of superstition, fomentors of reaction, and unflinchingly burned the pestilential forests of error, planting healthy orchards in their place—denounced the wicked professor who had hidden a dictionary of ideograms under his bed—blew up the monstrous hives where the poison of ignorance was stored—drove tractors through the flimsy rituals of superstition—and then, hand in hand, led their fellow producer-consumers to join the March to the Stars.

Behind the glib and bloated rhetoric lay real suffering, real passion. On both sides. Sutty knew that. She was a child of violence, as Tong Ov had said. Still she found it hard to keep in mind, and bitterly ironical, that here it was all the reverse of what she had known, the negative: that here the believers weren't the persecutors but the persecuted.

But they were all true believers, both sides. Secular terrorists or holy terrorists, what difference?

The only thing she had found at all unusual in the endless propaganda from the Ministries of Information and Poetry was that the heroes of the exemplary tales usually came in pairs—a brother and sister, or a betrothed or married couple. If a sexual pair, heterosexual, always. The Akan government was obsessive in its detestation of 'deviance.' Tong had warned her about it as soon as she arrived: "We must conform. No discussion, no question is possible. Anything that can be seen and reported as a sexual advance to a person of the same sex is a capital offense. So tiresome, so sad. These poor people!" He sighed for the sufferings of bigots and puritans, the sufferings and cruelties.

She had scarcely needed his warning, since she had so little contact with people as individuals, but she had of course heeded it; and it had been an element of her early, severe disappointment, her discouragement. The old Akan usages and language she had learned on Earth had led her to think she was coming to a sexually easygoing society with little or no gender hierarchy. The society of her native corner of Earth had still been cramped by social and gender caste, further rigidified by Unist misogyny and intolerance. No place on Earth had been entirely out from under that shadow, not even the Pales. One of the reasons she had specialised in Aka, had learned the languages, was that she and Pao had read in the First Observers' reports that Akan society was not hierarchically gendered and that heterosexuality was not compulsory, not even privileged. But all that had changed, changed utterly, during the years of her flight from Earth to Aka. Arriving here, she had had to go back to circumspection, caution, self-suppression. And danger.

So, then, why did they all so promptly try to enlist her, to use her? She was scarcely a jewel in anybody's crown.

Tong's reasons were superficially plain: he'd jumped at the first chance to send somebody out unsupervised, and chose her because she knew the old writing and language and would know what she found when she found it. But if she found it, what was she supposed to do with it? It was contraband. Illicit goods. Anti-Corporation sedition. Tong had said she was right to delete the fragments of the old books from the ansible transmission. Yet now he wanted her to record such material?

As for the Monitor, he was playing power games. It must be a thrill for a middle-weight supervisor of cultural correctness to find a genuine alien, an authentic Observer of the

Ekumen, to give orders to: Don't talk to social parasites—
don't leave town without permission—report to the boss
man, me.

What about the Fertiliser? She could not shake the
impression that he knew who she was, and that his gift had
some meaning beyond courtesy to a stranger. No telling
what.

Given her ignorance, if she let any of them control her,
she might do harm. But if she tried to do anything bold and
decisive on her own, she would almost certainly do harm.
She must go slow, wait, watch, learn.

Tong had given her a code word to use in a message in
case of trouble: 'devolve.' But he hadn't really expected
trouble. The Akans loved their alien guests, the cows from
whom they milked the milk of high technology. They
wouldn't let her get into danger. She mustn't paralyse herself
with caution.

The Monitor's rumbling about brutal tribespeople was
bogey talk. Okzat-Ozkat was a safe, a touchingly safe place to
live. It was a small, poor, provincial city, dragged along in the
rough wake of Akan progress, far enough behind that it still
held tattered remnants of the old way of life—the old civilisation. Probably the Corporation had consented to let an offworlder come here because it was so very out of the way, a
harmless, picturesque bywater. Tong had sent her here to follow up a hunch or hope of finding under the monolithic,
univocal success story of modern Aka some traces of what the

Ekumen treasured: the singular character of a people, their way of being, their history. The Akan Corporation State wanted to forget, hide, ban, bury all that, and if she learned anything here, it would not please them. But the days of burying and burning alive were over. Weren't they? The Monitor would bluster and bully, but what could he do?

Nothing much to her. A good deal, perhaps, to those who talked to her.

Hold still, she told herself. Listen. Listen to what they have to tell.

The air was dry at this altitude, cold in the shadow, hot in the sun. She stopped at a cafeteria near the Teachers' College to buy a bottle of fruit juice and sat with it at a table outdoors. Cheery music, exhortations, news about crops, production statistics, health programs blared across the square from the loudspeakers as always. Somehow she had to learn to listen through that noise to what it hid, the meaning under it.

Was its ceaselessness its meaning? Were the Akans afraid of silence?

Nobody about her seemed to be afraid of anything. They were students in green-and-rust Education uniforms. Many had the padded cheekbones and delicate bone structure of the old street people here, but they were plump and shiny with youth and confidence, chattering and shouting across her without seeing her. Any woman over thirty was an alien to them.

They were eating the kind of food she had eaten in the

capital, high-protein, sweet-salt packaged stuff, and drinking akakafi, a native hot drink rebaptized with a semi-Terran name. The Corporation brand of akakafi was called Starbrew and was ubiquitous. Bittersweet, black, it contained a remarkable mixture of alkaloids, stimulants, and depressants. Sutty loathed the taste, and it made her tongue furry, but she had learned to swallow it, since sharing akakafi was one of the few rituals of social bonding the people of Dovza City allowed themselves, and therefore very important to them. "A cup of akakafi?" they cried as soon as you came into the house, the office, the meeting. To refuse was to offer a rebuff, even an insult. Much small talk centered around akakafi: where to go for the best powder (not Starbrew, of course), where it was grown and processed, how to brew it. People boasted about how many cups they drank a day, as if the mild addiction were somehow praiseworthy. These young Educators were drinking it by the liter.

She listened to them dutifully, hearing chatter about examinations, prize lists, vacation travel. Nobody talked about reading or course material except two students nearby arguing about teaching preschoolers to use the toilet. The boy insisted that shame was the best incentive. The girl said, "Wipe it up and smile," which annoyed the boy into giving quite a lecture on peer adjustment, ethical goal setting, and hygienic laxity.

Walking home, Sutty wondered if Aka was a guilt culture, a shame culture, or something all its own. How was it

that everybody in the world was willing to move in the same
direction, talk the same language, believe the same things?
Fear of being evil, or fear of being different?

There she was, back with fear. Her problem, not theirs.

Her crippled hostess was sitting in the doorway when she
got home. They greeted each other shyly with illegal civili-
ties. Making conversation, Sutty said, "I like the teas you
serve so much. Much better than akafi."

Iziezi didn't slap one hand down and the other across her
mouth, but her hands did move abruptly, and she said, "Ah,"
exactly as the Fertiliser had said it. Then, after a long pause,
cautiously, shortening the invented word, she said, "But akafi
comes from your country."

"Some people on Terra drink something like it. My
people don't."

Iziezi looked tense. The subject was evidently fraught.

If every topic was a minefield, there was nothing to do
but talk on through the blasts, Sutty thought. She said, "You
don't like it either?"

Iziezi screwed up her face. After a nervous silence she
said earnestly, "It's bad for people. It dries up the sap and dis-
orders the flow. People who drink akafi, you can see their
hands tremble and their heart jump. That's what they used to
say, anyhow. The old-time people. A long time ago. My
grandmother. Now everybody drinks it. It was one of those
old rules, you know. Not modern. Modern people like it."

Caution; confusion; conviction.

"I didn't like the breakfast tea at first, but then I did. What is it? What does it do?"

Iziezi's face smoothed out. "That's bezit. It starts the flow and reunites. It refreshes the liver a little, too."

"You're a . . . herb teacher," Sutty said, not knowing the word for herbalist.

"Ah!"

A small mine going off. A small warning.

"Herb teachers are respected and honored in my homeland," Sutty said. "Many of them are doctors."

Iziezi said nothing, but gradually her face smoothed out again.

As Sutty turned to enter the house, the crippled woman said, "I'm going to exercise class in a few minutes."

Exercises? Sutty thought, glancing at the immobile stickshins that hung from Iziezi's knees.

"If you haven't found a class and would care to come. . . ."

The Corporation was very strong on gymnastics. Everybody in Dovza City belonged to a gymnogroup and went to fitness classes. Several times a day brisk music and shouts of One! Two! blared from the loudspeakers, and whole factories and office buildings poured their producer-consumers out into streets and courtyards to jump and punch and bend and swing in vigorous unison. As a foreigner, Sutty had mostly succeeded in evading these groups; but she looked at Iziezi's worn face and said, "I'd like to come."

She went in to find a place of honor in her bathroom for the Fertiliser's beautiful pot and to change from leggings into loose pants. When she came back out, Iziezi was transferring herself on crutches to a small powered wheelchair, Corporation issue, Starflight model. Sutty praised its design. Iziezi said dismissively, "It's all right in flat places," and took off, jolting and lurching up the steep, uneven street. Sutty walked alongside, lending a hand when the chair bucked and stuck, which it did about every two meters. They arrived at a low building with windows under the eaves and a high double door. One flap had been red and the other blue, with some kind of red-and-blue cloud motif painted above, now showing ghostly pink and grey through coats of whitewash. Iziezi headed her chair straight for the doors and barged them open. Sutty followed.

It seemed pitch-black inside. Sutty was getting used to these transitions from inside dark to outside dazzle and back, but her eyes weren't. Just inside the door, Iziezi paused for Sutty to take her shoes off and set them on a shelf at the end of a dim row of shoes, all black canvas StarMarch issue, of course. Then Iziezi steered her chair at a fearless clip down a long ramp, parked it behind a bench, and levered herself around onto the bench. It seemed to be at the edge of a large matted area, beyond which all was velvet gloom.

Sutty was able to make out shadowy figures sitting here and there cross-legged on the mat. Near Iziezi on the bench sat a man with one leg. Iziezi got herself arranged, set down

her crutches, and looked up at Sutty. She made a little pat-
ting gesture at the mat near her. The door had opened briefly
as someone came in, and in the brief grey visibility, Sutty saw
Iziezi smile. It was a lovely and touching sight.

Sutty sat down on the mat cross-legged with her hands in
her lap. For a long time nothing else happened. It was, she
thought, certainly unlike any exercise class she had ever
seen, and far more to her taste. People came in silently, one
or two at a time. As her eyes adjusted fully, she saw the room
was vast. It must be almost entirely dug into the ground. Its
long, low windows, right up where the wall met the ceiling,
were of a thick bluish glass that let in only diffuse light. Above
them the ceiling went on up in a low dome or series of
arches; she could just make out dark, branching beams. She
restrained her curious eyes and tried to sit, breathe, and not
fall asleep.

Unfortunately, in her experience, sitting meditation and
sleep had always tended to converge. When the man sitting
nearest her began to swell and shrink like the ideograms on
the Fertiliser's shop wall, it roused only a dreamy interest in
her. Then, sitting up a little straighter, she saw that he was
raising his outstretched arms till the backs of his hands met
above his head and then lowering them in a very slow, regular breath-rhythm. Iziezi and some others were doing the
same, in more or less the same rhythm. The serene, sound-
less movements were like the pulsing of jellyfish in a dim
aquarium. Sutty joined the pulsation.

Other motions were introduced here and there, one at a time, all arm movements, all in slow breath-rhythm. There would be periods of rest, and then the peaceful swelling and shrinking—stretch and relax, pulse out, draw in—would begin again, first one vague figure then another. A soft, soft sound accompanied the movements, a wordless rhythmic murmur, breath-music seemingly without source. Across the room one figure grew slowly up and up, whitish, undulant: a man or woman was afoot, making the arm gestures while bending forward or back or sideways from the waist. Two or three others rose in the same bonelessly supple way and stood reaching and swaying, never lifting a foot from the ground, more than ever like rooted sea creatures, anemones, a kelp forest, while the almost inaudible, ceaseless chanting pulsed like the sea swell, lifting and sinking . . .

Light, noise—a hard, loud, white blast as if the roof had been blown off. Bare square bulbs glared dangling from dusty vaultings. Sutty sat aghast as all around her people leapt to their feet and began to prance, kick, do jumping jacks, while a harsh voice shouted, "One! Two! One! Two! One! Two!" She stared round at Iziezi, who sat on her bench, jerking like a marionette, punching the air with her fists, one, two, one, two. The one-legged man next to her shouted out the beat, slamming his crutch against the bench in time.

Catching Sutty's eye, Iziezi gestured, Up!

Sutty stood up, obedient but disgusted. To achieve such a

beautiful group meditation and then destroy it with this stupid muscle building—what kind of people were these?

Two women in blue and tan were striding down the ramp after a man in blue and tan. The Monitor. His eyes went straight to her.

She stood among the others, who were all motionless now, except for the quick rise and fall of breath.

Nobody said anything.

The ban on servile address, on greetings, goodbyes, any phrase acknowledging presence or departure, left holes in the texture of social process, gaps crossed only by a slight effort, a recurrent strain. City Akans had grown up with the artificiality and no doubt did not feel it, but Sutty still did, and it seemed these people did too. The stiff silence enforced by the three standing on the ramp put the others at a disadvantage. They had no way to defuse it. The one-legged man at last cleared his throat and said with some bravado, "We are performing hygienic aerobic exercises as prescribed in the *Health Manual for Producer-Consumers of the Corporation.*"

The two women with the Monitor looked at each other, bored, sour, I-told-you-so. The Monitor spoke to Sutty across the air between them as if no one else were there: "You came here to practice aerobics?"

"We have very similar exercises in my homeland," she said, her dismay and indignation concentrating itself on him in a burst of eloquence. "I'm very glad to find a group here to practice them with. Exercise is often most profitable when performed with a sincerely interested group. Or so we believe in my homeland on Terra. And of course I hope to learn new exercises from my kind hosts here."

The Monitor, with no acknowledgment of any kind except a moment's pause, turned and followed the blue-and-tan women up the ramp. The women went out. He turned and stood just inside the doors, watching.

"Continue!" the one-legged man shouted. "One! Two! One! Two!" Everybody punched and kicked and bounced furiously for the next five or ten minutes. Sutty's fury was genuine at first; then it boiled off with the silly exercises, and she wanted to laugh, to laugh off the shock.

She pushed Iziezi's chair up the ramp, found her shoes among the row of shoes. The Monitor still stood there. She smiled at him. "You should join us," she said.

His gaze was impersonal, appraising, entirely without response. The Corporation was looking at her.

She felt her face change, felt her eyes flick over him with dismissive incredulity as if seeing something small, uncouth, a petty monster. Wrong! wrong! But it was done. She was past him, outside in the cold evening air.

She kept hold of the chair back to help Iziezi zigzag bumpily down the street and to distract herself from the crazy surge of hatred the Monitor had roused in her. "I see what you mean about level ground," she said.

"There's no—level—ground," Iziezi jerked out, holding

on, but lifting one hand for a moment toward the vast verti-
calities of Silong, flaring white-gold over roofs and hills
already drowned in dusk.

Back in the front hallway of the inn, Sutty said, "I hope I
may join your exercise class again soon."

Iziezi made a gesture that might have been polite assent
or hopeless apology.

"I preferred the quieter part," Sutty said. Getting no
smile or response, she said, "I really would like to learn those
movements. They're beautiful. They felt as if they had a
meaning in them."

Iziezi still said nothing.

"Is there a book about them, maybe, that I could study?"
The question seemed absurdly cautious yet foolishly rash.

Iziezi pointed into the common sitting room, where a
vid/neareal monitor sat blank in one corner. Stacks of Corpo-
ration-issue tapes were piled next to it. In addition to the
manuals, which everybody got a new set of annually, new
tapes were frequently delivered to one's door, informative,
educational, admonitory, inspirational. Employees and students were frequently examined on them in regular and special sessions at work and in college. *Illness does not excuse
ignorance!* blared the rich Corporational voice over vids of
hospitalised workmen enthusiastically partissing in a neareal
about plastic molding. *Wealth is work and work is wealth!*
sang the chorus for the Capital-Labor instructional vid. Most
of the literature Sutty had studied consisted of pieces of this

kind in the poetic and inspirational style. She looked with malevolence at the piles of tapes.

"The health manual," Iziezi murmured vaguely.

"I was thinking of something I could read in my room at night. A book."

"Ah!" The mine went off very close this time. Then silence. "Yoz Sutty," the crippled woman whispered, "books . . ."

Silence, laden.

"I don't mean to put you at any risk."

Sutty found herself, ridiculously, whispering.

Iziezi shrugged. Her shrug said, Risk, so, everything's a risk.

"The Monitor seems to be following me."

Iziezi made a gesture that said, No, no. "They come often to the class. We have a person to watch the street, turn the lights on. Then we . . ." Tiredly, she punched the air, One! Two!

"Tell me the penalties, yoz Iziezi."

"For doing the old exercises? Get fined. Maybe lose your license. Maybe you just have to go to the Prefecture or the High School and study the manuals."

"For a book? Owning it, reading it?"

"An . . . old book?"

Sutty made the gesture that said, Yes.

Iziezi was reluctant to answer. She looked down. She said finally, in a whisper, "Maybe a lot of trouble."

Iziezi sat in her wheelchair. Sutty stood. The light had died out of the street entirely. High over the roofs the barrier wall of Silong glowed dull rust-orange. Above it, far and radiant, the peak still burned gold.

"I can read the old writing. I want to learn the old ways. But I don't want you to lose your inn license, yoz Iziezi. Send me to somebody who isn't her nephew's sole support."

"Akidan?" Iziezi said with new energy. "Oh, he'd take you right up to the Taproot!" Then she slapped one hand on the wheelchair arm and put the other over her mouth. "So much is forbidden," she said from behind her hand, with a glance up at Sutty that was almost sly.

"And forgotten?"

"People remember. . . . People know, yoz. But I don't know anything. My sister knew. She was educated. I'm not. I know some people who are . . . educated. . . . But how far do you want to go?"

"As far as my guides lead me in kindness," Sutty said. It was a phrase not from the *Advanced Exercises in Grammar for Barbarians* but from the fragment of a book, the damaged page that had had on it the picture of a man fishing from a bridge and four lines of a poem:

> *Where my guides lead me in kindness*
> *I follow, follow lightly,*
> *and there are no footprints*
> *in the dust behind us.*

"Ah," Iziezi said, not a land mine, but a long sigh.

FOUR

IF THE MONITOR was keeping her under observation, she could go nowhere, learn nothing, without getting people into trouble. Possibly getting into trouble herself. And he was here to watch her; he had said so, if she'd only listened. It had taken all this time to dawn upon her that Corporation officials didn't travel by boat. They flew in Corporation planes and helis. Her conviction of her own insignificance had kept her from understanding his presence and heeding his warning.

She hadn't listened to what Tong Ov told her either: like it or not, admit it or not, she was important. She was the presence of the Ekumen on Aka. And the Monitor had told her, and she hadn't listened, that the Corporation had authorised him to prevent the Ekumen—her—from investigating and revealing the continued existence of reactionary practices, rotten-corpse ideologies.

A dog in a graveyard, that's how he saw her. *Keep far the Dog that's friend to men, or with his nails he'll dig it up again. . . .*

"Your heritage is Anglo-Hindic." Uncle Hurree, with his wild white eyebrows and his sad, fiery eyes. "You must know Shakespeare and the Upanishads, Sutty. You must know the Gita and the Lake Poets."

She did. She knew too many poets. She knew more poets, more poetry, she knew more grief, she knew more than anybody needed to know. So she had sought to be ignorant. To come to a place where she didn't know anything. She had succeeded beyond all expectation.

After long pondering in her peaceful room, long indecision and anxiety, some moments of despair, she sent her first report to Tong Ov—and incidentally to the Office of Peace and Surveillance, the Sociocultural Ministry, and whatever other bureaus of the Corporation intercepted everything that came to Tong's office. It took her two days to write two pages. She described her boat journey, the scenery, the city. She mentioned the excellent food and fine mountain air. She requested a prolongation of her holiday, which had proved both enjoyable and educational, though hampered by the well-intended but overprotective zeal of an official who thought it necessary to insulate her from conversations and interactions with the local people.

The corporative government of Aka, while driven to control everyone and everything, also wanted very much to please and impress their visitors from the Ekumen. To *measure up*, as Uncle Hurree would have said. The Envoy was expert at using that second motive to limit the first; but her message could cause him problems. They had let him send an Observer into a 'primitive' area, but they had sent an observer of their own to observe the Observer.

She waited for Tong's reply, increasingly certain that he would be forced to call her back to the capital. The thought of Dovza City made her realise how much she did not want to leave the little city, the high country. For three days she went on hikes out into the farmlands and up along the bank of the glacier-blue, rowdy young river, sketched Silong above the curlicued roofs of Okzat-Ozkat, entered Iziezi's recipes for her exquisite food in her noter but did not return to 'exercise class' with her, talked with Akidan about his schoolwork and sports but did not talk to any strangers or street people, was studiously touristic and innocuous.

Since she came to Okzat-Ozkat, she had slept well, without the long memory-excursions that had broken her nights in Dovza City; but during this time of waiting she woke every night in the depths of the darkness and was back in the Pale.

The first night, she was in the tiny living room of her parents' flat, watching Dalzul on the neareal. Father, a neurologist, abominated vr-proprios. "Lying to the body is worse than torturing it," he growled, looking like Uncle Hurree. He had long ago disconnected the vr modules from their set, so that it functioned merely as a holo TV. Having grown up in the village with no commtech but radios and an ancient 2D television in the town meeting hall, Sutty didn't miss vr-prop. She had been studying, but turned her chair round to see the Envoy of the Ekumen standing on the balcony of the Sanctum, flanked by the white-robed Fathers.

The Fathers' mirror masks reflected the immense throng, hundreds of thousands of people gathered in the Great Square, as a tiny dappling. Sunlight shone on Dalzul's bright, amazing hair. The Angel, they called him now, God's Herald, the Divine Messenger. Mother scoffed and grumbled at such terms, but she watched him as intently, listened to his words as devoutly as any Unist, as anybody, everybody in the world. How did Dalzul bring hope to the faithful and hope to the unbelievers at the same time, in the same words?

"I want to distrust him," Mother said. "But I can't. He is going to do it—to put the Meliorist Fathers into power. Incredible! He is going to set us free."

Sutty had no trouble believing it. She knew, from Uncle Hurree and from school and from her own apparently innate conviction, that the Rule of the Fathers under which she had lived all her life had been a fit of madness. Unism was a panic response to the great famines and epidemics, a spasm of global guilt and hysterical expiation, which had been working itself into its final orgy of violence when Dalzul the "Angel" came from "Heaven" and with his magic oratory turned all that zeal from destruction to lovingkindness, from mass murder to mild embrace. A matter of timing; a tip of the balance. Wise with the wisdom of Hainish teachers who had been through such episodes a thousand times in their endless history, canny as his white Terran ancestors who had convinced everybody else on Earth that their way was the only way, Dalzul had only to set his finger on the scales to turn blind, bigoted hatred into blind, universal love. And now peace and reason would return, and Terra would regain her place among the peaceful, reasonable worlds of the Ekumen. Sutty was twenty-three and had no trouble believing it at all.

Freedom Day, the day they opened the Pale: the restrictions on unbelievers lifted, all the restrictions on communications, books, women's clothing, travel, worship and nonworship, everything. The people of the Pale came pouring out of the shops and houses, the high schools and the training schools into the rainy streets of Vancouver.

They didn't know what to do, really, they had lived so long silent, demure, cautious, humble, while the Fathers preached and ruled and ranted and the Officers of the Faith confiscated, censored, threatened, punished. It had always been the faithful who gathered in huge crowds, shouted praises, sang songs, celebrated, marched here and marched there, while the unbelievers lay low and talked soft. But the rain let up, and people brought guitars and sitars and saxophones out into the streets and squares and began playing music and dancing. The sun came out, low and gold under big clouds, and they went on dancing the joyous dances of unbelief. In McKenzie Square there was a girl leading a round dance, black heavy glossy hair, ivory skin, Sino-Canadian, laughing, a noisy, laughing girl, too loud, brassy, self-confident, but Sutty joined her round dance because the people in it were having such a good time and the boy playing the concertina made such terrific music. She and the black-haired girl came face to face in some figure of the dance they had just invented. They took each other's hands. One laughed, and the other laughed. They never let go of each other's hands all night.

From that memory Sutty plunged soft and straight into sleep, the untroubled sleep she almost always had in this high, quiet room.

Next day she hiked a long way up the river, came back late and tired. She ate with Iziezi, read a while, unrolled her bed.

As soon as she turned the light off and lay down, she was back in Vancouver, the day after freedom.

They had gone for a walk up above the city in New Stanley Park, the two of them. There were still some big trees there, enormous trees from before the pollution. Firs, Pao said. Douglas firs, and spruce, they were called. Once the mountains had been black with them. "Black with them!" she said in her husky, unmodulated voice, and Sutty saw the great black forests, the heavy, glossy black hair.

"You grew up here?" she asked, for they had everything to learn about each other, and Pao said, "Yes I did, and now I want to get out!"

"Where to?"

"Hain, Ve, Chiffewar, Werel, Yeowe-Werel, Gethen, Urras-Anarres, O!"

"O, O, O!" Sutty crowed, laughing and half crying to hear her own litany, her secret mantra shouted out loud. "I do too! I will, I will, I'm going!"

"Are you in training?"

"Third year."

"I just started."

"Catch up!" Sutty said.

And Pao almost did so. She got through three years of work in two. Sutty graduated after the first of those years and stayed on the second as a graduate associate, teaching deep grammar and Hainish to beginning students. When she went to the Ekumenical School in Valparaíso, she and Pao would be apart only eight months; and she would fly back up to Vancouver for the December holiday, so they'd only actually be separated for four months and then four months again, and then together, together all the way through the Ekumenical School, and all the rest of their lives, all over the Known Worlds. "We'll be making love on a world nobody even knows the name of now, a thousand years from now!" Pao said, and laughed her lovely chortling laugh that started down inside her belly, in what she called her tan-tien-tummy, and ended up rocking her to and fro. She loved to laugh, she loved to tell jokes and be told them. Sometimes she laughed out loud in her sleep. Sutty would feel and hear the soft laughter in the darkness, and in the morning Pao would explain that her dreams had been so funny, and laugh again trying to tell the funny dreams.

They lived in the flat they'd found and moved into two weeks after freedom, the dear grubby basement flat on Souché Street, Sushi Street because there were three Japanese restaurants on it. They had two rooms: one with wall-to-wall futons, one with the stove, the sink, and the upright piano with four dead keys that came with the flat because it was too far gone to repair and too expensive to move. Pao played crashing waltzes with holes in them while Sutty cooked bhaigan tamatar. Sutty recited the poems of Esnanaridaratha of Darranda and filched almonds while Pao fried rice. A mouse gave birth to infant mice in the storage cabinet. Long discussions about what to do about the infant mice ensued. Ethnic slurs were exchanged: the ruthlessness of the Chinese, who treated animals as insentient, the wickedness of the Hindus, who fed sacred cows and let children starve. "I will not live with mice!" Pao shouted. "I will not live with a murderer!" Sutty shouted back. The infant mice became adolescents and began making forays. Sutty bought a secondhand box trap. They baited it with tofu. They caught the mice one by one and released them in New Stanley Park.

The mother mouse was the last to be caught, and when they released her they sang:

> *God will bless thee, loving mother*
> *Of thy faithful husband's child,*
> *Cling to him and know no other,*
> *Living pure and undefiled.*

Pao knew a lot of Unist hymns, and had one for most occasions.

Sutty got the flu. Flu was a frightening thing, so many strains of it were fatal. She remembered vividly her terror, standing in the crowded streetcar while the headache got worse and worse, and when she got home and couldn't focus her eyes on Pao's face. Pao cared for her night and day and when the fever went down made her drink Chinese medicinal teas that tasted like piss and mildew. She was weak for days and days, lying there on the futons staring at the dingy ceiling, weak and stupid, peaceful, coming back to life.

But in that epidemic little Aunty found her way back to the village. The first time Sutty was strong enough to visit home, it was strange to be there with Mother and Father and not with Aunty. She kept turning her head, thinking Aunty was standing in the doorway or sitting in her chair in the other room in her ragged blanket cocoon. Mother gave Sutty Aunty's bangles, the six everyday brass ones, the two gold

ones for dressing up, tiny, frail circlets through which Sutty's
hands would never pass. She gave them to Lakshmi for her
baby girl to wear when she got bigger. "Don't hold on to
things, they weigh you down. Keep in your head what's worth
keeping," Uncle Hurree had said, preaching what he'd had to
practice; but Sutty kept the red-and-orange saree of cotton
gauze, which folded up into nothing and could not weigh
her down. It was in the bottom of her suitcase here, in Okzat-
Ozkat. Someday maybe she would show it to Iziezi. Tell her
about Aunty. Show her how you wore a saree. Most women
enjoyed that and liked to try it on themselves. Pao had tried
on Sutty's old grey-and-silver saree once, to entertain Sutty
while she was convalescing, but she said it felt too much like
skirts, which of course she had been forced to wear in public
all her life because of the Unist clothing laws, and she
couldn't get the trick of securing the top. "My tits are going to
pop out!" she cried, and then, encouraging them to do so,
had performed a remarkable version of what she called
Indian classical dance all over the futons.

Sutty had been frightened again, very badly frightened,
when she discovered that everything she'd learned in the
months before she got the flu—the Ekumenical history, the
poems she'd memorised, even simple words of Hainish she
had known for years—seemed to have been wiped out. "What
will I do, what will I do, if I can't keep things even in my
head?" she whispered to Pao, when she finally broke down
and confessed to the terror that had been tormenting her for a

week. Pao hadn't comforted her much, just let her tell her fear
and misery, and finally said, "I think that will wear off. I think
you'll find it all coming back." And of course she was right.
Talking about it changed it. The next day, as Sutty was riding
the streetcar, the opening lines of *The Terraces of Darranda*
suddenly flowered out in her mind like great fireworks, the
marvelous impetuous orderly fiery words; and she knew that
all the other words were there, not lost, waiting in the darkness, ready to come when she called them. She bought a huge
bunch of daisies and took them home for Pao. They put them
in the one vase they had, black plastic, and they looked like
Pao, black and white and gold. With the vision of those flowers an intense and complete awareness of Pao's body and presence filled her now, here in the high quiet room on another
world, as it had filled her constantly there, then, when she was
with Pao, and when she wasn't with her, but there was no time
that they weren't together, no time that they were truly apart,
not even that long, long flight down all the coast of the Amer-
icas had separated them. Nothing had separated them. *Let me
not to the marriage of true minds admit impediment . . .* "O my
true mind," she whispered in the dark, and felt the warm arms
holding her before she slept.

Tong Ov's brief reply came, a printout, received at a bureau of
the District Prefecture and hand-delivered, after inspection of

her ZIL bracelet, by a uniformed messenger. *Observer Sutty Dass: Consider your holiday the beginning of a field trip. Continue research and recording personal observations as you see fit.*

So much for the Monitor! Surprised and jubilant, Sutty went outdoors to look up at the bannered peak of Silong and think where to start.

She had gathered in her mind innumerable things to learn about: the meditation exercises; the double-cloud doors, which she had found all over the city, always white-washed or painted over; the inscriptions in shops; the tree metaphors she kept hearing in talk about food or health or anything to do with the body; the possible existence of banned books; the certain existence of a web or net of information, subtler than the electronic one and uncontrolled by the Corporation, that kept people all over the city in touch and aware at all times of, for instance, Sutty: who she was, where she was, what she wanted. She saw this awareness in the eyes of street people, shopkeepers, schoolchildren, the old women who dug in the little gardens, the old men who sat in the sun on barrels on street corners. She felt it as unin-vasive, as if she walked among faint lines of guidance, not bonds, not constraints, but reassurances. That she had not first entered either Iziezi's or the Fertiliser's door entirely by chance now seemed probable, though she could not explain it, and acceptable, though she did not know why.

Now that she was free, she wanted to go back to the Fertiliser's shop. She went up into the hills of the city, began to climb that narrow street. Halfway up it she came face to face with the Monitor.

Released from concern about either obeying or evading him, she looked at him as she had at first on the river journey, not as the object of bureaucratic control looks at the bureaucrat, but humanly. He had a straight back and good features, though ambition, anxiety, authority had made his face hard, tight. Nobody starts out that way, Sutty thought. There are no hard babies. Magnanimous, she greeted him, "Good morning, Monitor!"

Her cheery, foolish voice rang in her own ears. Wrong, wrong. To him such a greeting was mere provocation. He stood silent, facing her.

He cleared his throat and said, "I have been ordered to withdraw my request to you to inform my office of your contacts and travel plans. Since you did not comply with it, I attempted to keep some protective surveillance over you. I am informed that you complained of this. I apologise for any annoyance or inconvenience caused you by myself or my staff."

His tone was cold and dour but he had some dignity, and Sutty, ashamed, said, "No—I'm sorry, I—"

"I warn you," he said, paying no attention, his voice more intense, "that there are people here who intend to use you for their own ends. These people are not picturesque relics of a time gone by. They are not harmless. They are vicious. They are the dregs of a deadly poison—the drug that stupefied my people for ten thousand years. They seek to drag us back into that paralysis, that mindless barbarism. They may treat you kindly, but I tell you they are ruthless. You are a prize to them. They'll flatter you, teach you lies, promise you miracles. They are the enemies of truth, of science. Their so-called knowledge is rant, superstition, poetry. Their practices are illegal, their books and rites are banned, and you know that. Do not put my people into the painful position of finding a scientist of the Ekumen in possession of illegal materials—participating in obscene, unlawful rites. I ask this of you—as a scientist of the Ekumen—" He had begun to stammer, groping for words.

Sutty looked at him, finding his emotion unnerving, grotesque. She said drily, "I am not a scientist. I read poetry. And you need not tell me the evils religion can do. I know them."

"No," he said, "you do not." His hands clenched and unclenched. "You know nothing of what we were. How far we have come. We will never go back to barbarism."

"Do you know anything at all about my world?" she said with incredulous scorn. Then none of this talk seemed worthwhile to her, and she only wanted to get away from the zealot. "I assure you that no representative of the Ekumen will interfere in Akan concerns unless explicitly asked to do so," she said.

He looked straight at her and spoke with extraordinary passion. "Do not betray us!"

"I have no intention —"

He turned his head aside as if in denial or pain. Abruptly he walked on past her, down the street.

She felt a wave of hatred for him that frightened her.

She turned and went on, telling herself that she should be sorry for him. He was sincere. Most bigots are sincere. The stupid, arrogant fool, trying to tell her that religion was dangerous! But he was merely parroting Dovzan propaganda. Trying to frighten her, angry because his superiors had put him in the wrong. That he couldn't control her was so intolerable to him that he'd lost control of himself. There was absolutely no need to think about him any more.

She walked on up the street to the little shop to ask the Fertiliser what the double-cloud doors were, as she had intended.

When she entered, the high dim room with its word-covered walls seemed part of a different reality altogether. She stood there for a minute, letting that reality become hers. She looked up at the inscription: *In the dark cloud's descent from sky the twice-forked lightning-tree grows up from earth.*

The elegant little pot the Fertiliser had given her bore a motif that she had taken to be a stylised shrub or tree before she saw that it might be a variation on the cloud-door shape. She had sketched the design from the pot. When the Fertiliser materialised from the dark backward and abysm of his shop, she put her sketch down on the counter and said, "Please, yoz, can you tell me what this design is?"

He studied the drawing. He observed in his thin, dry voice, "It's a very pretty drawing."

"It's from the gift you gave me. Has the design a meaning, a significance?"

"Why do you ask, yoz?"

"I'm interested in old things. Old words, old ways."

He watched her with age-faded eyes and said nothing.

"Your government"—she used the old word, *biedins*, 'system of officials,' rather than the modern *vizdestit*, 'joint business' or 'corporation'—"Your government, I know, prefers that its people learn new ways, not dwelling on their past." Again she used the old word for people, not *riyingdutey*, producer-consumers. "But the historians of the Ekumen are interested in everything that our member worlds have to teach, and we believe that a useful knowledge of the present is rooted in the past."

The Fertiliser listened, affably impassive.

She forged ahead. "I've been asked by the official senior to me in the capital to learn what I can about some of the old ways that no longer exist in the capital, the arts and beliefs and customs that flourished on Aka before my people came here. I've received assurance from a Sociocultural Monitor that his office won't interfere with my studies." She said the last sentence with a certain vengeful relish. She still felt shaken, sore, from her confrontation with the Monitor. But the peacefulness in this place, the dim air, the faint scents, the half-visible ancient writings, made all that seem far away.

A pause. The old man's thin forefinger hovered over the design she had drawn. "We do not see the roots," he said.

She listened.

"The trunk of the tree," he said, indicating the element of the design that, in a building, was the double-leafed door. "The branches and foliage of the tree, the crown of leaves." He indicated the five-lobed 'cloud' that rose above the trunk. "Also this is the body, you see, yoz." He touched his own hips and sides, patted his head with a certain leafy motion of the fingers, and smiled a little. "The body is the body of the world. The world's body is my body. So, then, the one makes two." His finger showed where the trunk divided. "And the two bear each three branches, that rejoin, making five." His finger moved to the five lobes of foliage. "And the five bear the myriad, the leaves and flowers that die and return, return and die. The beings, creatures, stars. The being that can be told. But we don't see the roots. We cannot tell them."

"The roots are in the ground . . . ?"

"The mountain is the root." He made a beautiful formal gesture, the backs of his fingers touching at the tip to shape a peak, then moving in to touch his breast over his heart.

"The mountain is the root," she repeated. "These are mysteries."

He was silent.

"Can you tell me more? Tell me about the two, and the three, and the five, yoz."

"These are things that take a long time to tell, yoz."

"My time is all for listening. But I don't want to waste yours, or intrude on it. Or ask you to tell me anything you don't want to tell me, anything better kept secret."

"Everything's kept secret now," he said in that papery voice. "And yet it's all in plain sight." He looked round at the cases of little drawers and the walls above them entirely covered with words, charms, poems, formulas. Today in Sutty's eyes the ideograms did not swell and shrink, did not breathe, but rested motionless on the high, dim walls. "But to so many they aren't words, only old scratches. So the police leave them alone. . . . In my mother's time, all children could read. They could begin to read the story. The telling never stopped. In the forests and the mountains, in the villages and the cities, they were telling the story, telling it aloud, reading it aloud. Yet it was all secret then too. The mystery of the beginning, of the roots of the world, the dark. The grave, yoz. Where it begins."

So her education began. Though later she thought it had truly begun when she sat at the little tray-table in her room in Iziezi's house, with the first taste of that food on her tongue.

———

One of the historians of Darranda said: *To learn a belief without belief is to sing a song without the tune.*

A yielding, an obedience, a willingness to accept these notes as the right notes, this pattern as the true pattern, is the

essential gesture of performance, translation, and understanding. The gesture need not be permanent, a lasting posture of the mind or heart; yet it is not false. It is more than the
suspension of disbelief needed to watch a play, yet less than a
conversion. It is a position, a posture in the dance. So Sutty's
teachers, gathered from many worlds to the city Valparaíso de
Chile, had taught her, and she had had no cause to question
their teaching.

She had come to Aka to learn how to sing this world's
tune, to dance its dance; and at last, she thought, away from
the city's endless noise, she was beginning to hear the music
and to learn how to move to it.

Day after day she recorded her notes, observations that
stumbled over each other, contradicted, amplified, back-
tracked, speculated, a wild profusion of information on all
sorts of subjects, a jumbled and jigsawed map that for all its
complexity represented only a rough sketch of one corner of
the vastness she had to explore: a way of thinking and living
developed and elaborated over thousands of years by the vast
majority of human beings on this world, an enormous interlocking system of symbols, metaphors, correspondences, the-
ories, cosmology, cooking, calisthenics, physics, metaphysics,
metallurgy, medicine, physiology, psychology, alchemy,
chemistry, calligraphy, numerology, herbalism, diet, legend,
parable, poetry, history, and story.

In this vast mental wilderness she looked for paths and
signs, institutions that could be described, ideas that could be

defined. Instinctively she avoided great cloudy concepts and sought tangibilities, such as architecture. The buildings in Okzat-Ozkat with the double doors that represented the Tree had been temples, *umyazu*, a word now banned, a nonword. Nonwords were useful markers of paths that might lead through the wilderness. Was 'temple' the best translation? What had gone on in the umyazu?

Well, people said, people used to go there and listen.

To what?

Oh, well, the stories, you know.

Who told the stories?

Oh, the maz did. They lived there. Some of them.

Sutty gathered that the umyazu had been something like monasteries, something like churches, and very much like libraries: places where professionals gathered and kept books and people came to learn to read them, to read them, and to hear them read. In richer areas, there had been great, rich umyazu, to which people went on pilgrimage to see the treasures of the library and 'hear the Telling.' These had all been destroyed, pulled down or blown up, except the oldest and most famous of all, the Golden Mountain, far to the east.

From an official neareal she had partissed in while she was in Dovza City, she knew that the Golden Mountain had been made into a Corporate Site for the worship of the God of Reason: an artificial cult that had no existence except at this tourist center and in slogans and vague pronouncements of the Corporation. The Golden Mountain had been gutted, first, however. The neareal showed scenes of books being removed from a great underground archive by machinery, big scoops shoveling books up like dirt into dump trucks, backhoes ramming and scraping books into a landfill. The viewer of the neareal partissed in the operation of one of these machines, while lively, bouncy music played. Sutty had stopped the neareal in the midst of this scene and disconnected the vr-proprios from the set. After that she had watched and listened to Corporation neareals but never partissed in one again, though she reconnected the vr-p modules every day when she left her special research cubicle at the Central Ministry of Poetry and Art.

Memories such as that inclined her to some sympathy with this religion, or whatever it was she was studying, but caution and suspicion balanced her view. It was her job to avoid opinion and theory, stick to evidence and observation, listen and record what she was told.

Despite the fact that it was all banned, all illicit, people talked to her quite freely, trustfully answering her questions. She had no trouble finding out about the yearlong and lifelong cycles and patterns of feasts, fasts, indulgences, abstinences, passages, festivals. These observances, which seemed in a general way to resemble the practices of most of the religions she knew anything about, were now of course subterranean, hidden away, or so intricately and unobtrusively woven into the fabric of ordinary life that the Monitors of the Sociocultural Office couldn't put their finger on any act and say, "This is forbidden."

The menus of the little restaurants for working people in Okzat-Ozkat were a nice example of this kind of obscurely flourishing survival of illicit practices. The menu was written up in the modern alphabet on a board at the door. Along with akakafi, it featured the foods produced by the Corporation and advertised, distributed, and sold all over Aka by the Bureau of Public Health and Nutrition: produce from the great agrifactories, high-protein, vitamin-enriched, packaged, needing only heating. The restaurants kept some of these things in stock, freeze-dried, canned, or frozen, and a few people ordered them. Most people who came to these little places ordered nothing. They sat down, greeted the waiter, and waited to be served the fresh food and drink that was appropriate to the day, the time of day, the season, and the weather, according to an immemorial theory and practice of diet, the goal of which was to live long and well with a good digestion. Or with a peaceful heart. The two phrases were the same in Rangma, the local language.

In her noter in one of her long evening recording sessions, late in the autumn, sitting on the red rug in her quiet room, she defined the Akan system as a religion-philosophy of the type of Buddhism or Taoism, which she had learned about during her Terran education: what the Hainish, with their passion for lists and categories, called a religion of process. "There are no native Akan words for God, gods, the divine," she told her noter. "The Corporation bureaucrats made up a word for God and installed state theism when they learned that a concept of deity was important on the worlds they took as models. They saw that religion is a useful tool for those in power. But there was no native theism or deism here. On Aka, *god* is a word without referent. No capital letters. No creator, only creation. No eternal father to reward and punish, justify injustice, ordain cruelty, offer salvation. Eternity not an endpoint but a continuity. Primal division of being into material and spiritual only as two-as-one, or one in two aspects. No hierarchy of Nature and Supernatural. No binary Dark/Light, Evil/Good, or Body/Soul. No afterlife, no rebirth, no immortal disembodied or reincarnated soul. No heavens, no hells. The Akan system is a spiritual discipline with spiritual goals, but they're exactly the same goals it seeks for bodily and ethical well-being. Right action is its own end. Dharma without karma."

She had arrived at a definition of Akan religion. For a minute she was perfectly satisfied with it and with herself.

Then she found she was thinking about a group of myths that Ottiar Uming had been telling. The central figure, Ezid, a strange, romantic character who appeared sometimes as a beautiful, gentle young man and sometimes as a beautiful, fearless young woman, was called "the Immortal." She added a note: "What about 'Immortal Ezid'? Does this imply belief in an afterlife? Is Ezid one person, two, or many? *Immortal/*

living-forever seems to mean: intense, repeated many times, famous, perhaps also a special 'educated' meaning: in perfect bodily/spiritual health, living wisely. Check this."

Again and again in her notes, after every conclusion: *Check this.* Conclusions led to new beginnings. Terms changed, were corrected, recorrected. Before long she became unhappy with her definition of the system as a religion; it seemed not incorrect, but not wholly adequate. The term *philosophy* was even less adequate. She went back to calling it the system, the Great System. Later she called it the Forest, because she learned that in ancient times it had been called the way through the forest. She called it the Mountain when she found that some of her teachers called what they taught her the way to the mountain. She ended up calling it the Telling. But that was after she came to know Maz Elyed.

She had long debates with her noter about whether any word in Dovzan, or in the older and partly non-Dovzan vocabulary used by 'educated' people, could be said to mean sacred or holy. There were words she translated as power, mystery, not-controlled-by-people, part-of-harmony. These terms were never reserved for a certain place or type of action. Rather it appeared that in the old Akan way of thinking any place, any act, if properly perceived, was actually mysterious and powerful, potentially sacred. And perception seemed to involve description — telling about the place, or the act, or the event, or the person. Talking about it, making it into a story.

But these stories weren't gospel. They weren't Truth. They weren't essays at the truth. Glances, glimpses of sacredness. One was not asked to believe, only to listen.

"Well, that's how I learned the story," they would say, having told a parable or recounted a historical episode or recited an ancient and familiar legend. "Well, that's the way this telling goes."

The holy people in their stories achieved holiness, if that was what it was, by all kinds of different means, none of which seemed particularly holy to Sutty. There were no rules, such as poverty chastity obedience, or exchanging one's worldly goods for a wooden begging bowl, or reclusion on a mountaintop. Some of the heroes and famous maz in the stories were flamboyantly rich; their virtue had apparently consisted in generosity—building great beautiful umyazu to house their treasures, or going on processions with hundreds of companions all mounted on eberdin with silver harnesses. Some of the heroes were warriors, some were powerful leaders, some were shoemakers, some were shopkeepers. Some of the holy people in the stories were passionate lovers, and the story was about their passion. A lot of them were couples. There were no rules. There was always an alternative. The story-tellers, when they commented on the legends and histories they told, might point out that that had been a good way or a right way of doing something, but they never talked about *the* right way. And good was an adjective, always: good food, good health, good sex, good weather. No capital letters. Good or Evil as entities, warring powers, never.

This system wasn't a religion at all, Sutty told her noter with increasing enthusiasm. Of course it had a spiritual dimension. In fact, it *was* the spiritual dimension of life for those who lived it. But religion as an institution demanding belief and claiming authority, religion as a community shaped by a knowledge of foreign deities or competing institutions, had never existed on Aka.

Until, perhaps, the present time.

Aka's habitable lands were a single huge continent with an immensely long archipelago off its eastern coast. Dovza was the farthest southwestern region of the great continent. Undivided by oceans, the Akans were physically all of one type with slight local variations. All the Observers had remarked on this, all had pointed out the ethnic homogeneity, the lack of societal and cultural diversity, but none of them had quite realised that among the Akans there *were no foreigners.* There had never been any foreigners, until the ships from the Ekumen landed.

It was a simple fact, but one remarkably difficult for the Terran mind to comprehend. No aliens. No others, in the deadly sense of otherness that existed on Terra, the implacable division between tribes, the arbitrary and impassable borders, the ethnic hatreds cherished over centuries and millennia. 'The people' here meant not *my* people, but people—everybody, humanity. 'Barbarian' didn't mean an incomprehensible outlander, but an uneducated person. On Aka, all competition was familial. All wars were civil wars.

One of the great epics Sutty was now recording in pieces and fragments concerned a long-running and bloody feud over a fertile valley, which began as a quarrel between a brother and sister over inheritance. Struggles between regions and city-states for economic dominance had gone on all through Akan history, flaring often into armed conflict. But these wars and feuds had been fought by professional soldiers, on battlefields. It was a very rare thing, and treated in the histories and annals as shamefully, punishably wrong, for soldiers to destroy cities or farmlands or to hurt civilians. Akans fought each other out of greed and ambition for power, not out of hatred and not in the name of a belief. They fought by the rules. They had the same rules. They were one people. Their system of thought and way of life had been universal. They had all sung one tune, though in many voices.

Much of this communality, Sutty thought, had depended on the writing. Before the Dovzan cultural revolution there had been several major languages and innumerable dialects, but they had all used the same ideograms, mutually intelligible to all. Clumsy and archaic as nonalphabetic scripts were in some respects, they could bond and preserve, as Chinese ideograms had done on Earth, a great diversity of languages and dialects; and they made texts written thousands of years ago readable without translation even though the sounds of the words had changed out of all recognition. Indeed, to the Dovzan reformers, that may have been the chief reason for getting rid of the old script: it was not only an impediment to progress but an actively conservative force. It kept the past alive.

In Dovza City she had met nobody who could, or who admitted they could, read the old writing. Her few early questions concerning it met with such disapproval and blank rejection that she promptly learned not to mention the fact that she could read it. And the officials dealing with her never asked. The old writing had not been used for decades; it probably never occurred to them that, through the accident of time lapse during space travel, it had been the writing she learned.

She had not been entirely foolish to wonder, there in Dovza City, if she might actually be the only person in the world who could now read it, and not entirely foolish to be frightened by the thought. If she carried the entire history of a people, not her own people, in her head, then if she forgot one word, one character, one diacritical mark, that much of all those lives, all those centuries of thought and feeling, would be lost forever. . . .

It had been a vast relief to her to find, here in Okzat-Ozkat, many people, old and young, even children, carrying and sharing that precious cargo. Most could read and write a few dozen characters, or a few hundred, and many went on

to full literacy. In the Corporation schools, children learned
the Hainish-derived alphabet and were educated as producer-consumers; at home or in illicit classes in little rooms
behind a shop, a workshop, a warehouse, they learned the
ideograms. They practiced writing the characters on small
blackboards that could be wiped clean with a stroke. Their
teachers were working people, householders, shopkeepers,
common people of the city.

These teachers of the old language and the old way, the
'educated people,' were called maz. Yoz was a term indicating respectful equality; maz as an address indicated increased
respect. As a title or a noun, it meant, as Sutty began to
understand it, a function or profession that wasn't definable
as priest, teacher, doctor, or scholar, but contained aspects of
them all.

All the maz Sutty met, and as the weeks went on she met
most of the maz in Okzat-Ozkat, lived in more or less comfortable poverty. Usually they had a trade or job to supple-
ment what they were paid as maz for teaching, dispensing
medicine and counsel on diet and health, performing certain
ceremonies such as marriage and burial, and reading and
talking in the evening meetings, the tellings. The maz were
poor, not because the old way was dying or was treasured
only by the old, but because the people who paid them were
poor. This was a hard-bitten little city, marginal, without
wealth. But the people supported their maz, paid for their
teaching "by the word," as they said. They came to the house

of one maz or another in the evening to listen to the stories
and the discussions, paying regular fees in copper money,
small paper bills. There was no shame in the transaction on
either side, no hypocrisy of 'donation': cash was paid for value
received.

Many children were brought along in the evening to the
tellings, to which they listened, more or less, or fell quietly
asleep. No fee was charged for children until they were fifteen or so, when they began to pay the same fees as adults.
Adolescents favored the sessions of certain maz who specialised in reciting or reading epics and romances, such as
The Valley War and the tales of Ezid the Beautiful. Exercise
classes of the more vigorous and martial kind were full of
young men and women.

The maz, however, were mostly middle-aged or old,
again not because they were dying out as a group, but
because, as they said, it took a lifetime to learn how to walk in
the forest.

Sutty wanted to find out why the task of becoming educated was interminable; but the task of finding out seemed to
be interminable itself. What was it these people believed?
What was it they held sacred? She kept looking for the core of
the matter, the words at the heart of the Telling, the holy books
to study and memorise. She found them, but not it. No bible.
No koran. Dozens of upanishads, a million sutras. Every maz
gave her something else to read. Already she had read or heard
countless texts, written, oral, both written and oral, many or

most of them existing in more than one mode and more than one version. The subject matter of the tellings seemed to be endless, even now, when so much had been destroyed.

Early in the winter she thought she had found the central texts of the system in a series of poems and treatises called *The Arbor*. All the maz spoke of it with great respect, all of them quoted from it. She spent weeks studying it. As well as she could determine, it had mostly been written between fifteen hundred and a thousand years ago in the central region of the continent during a period of material prosperity and artistic and intellectual ferment. It was a vast compendium of sophisticated philosophical reasonings on being and becoming, form and chaos, mystical meditations on the Making and the Made, and beautiful, difficult, metaphysical poems concerning the One that is Two, the Two that are One, all interconnected, illuminated, and complicated by the commentaries and marginalia of all the centuries since. Uncle Hurree's niece, the scholar-pedant, rushed exulting into that jungle of significances, willing to be lost there for years. She was brought back to daylight only by her conscience, which trailed along carrying the heavy baggage of common sense, nagging: But this isn't the Telling, this is just a part of it, just a *small* part of it. . . .

Conscience finally got decisive help in its task from Maz Oryen Viya, who mentioned that the text of *The Arbor* that Sutty had been coming to study at his house every day for a month was only a portion of, and in many places entirely different from, a text he had seen many years ago in a great umyazu in Amareza.

There was no correct text. There was no standard version. Of anything. There was not one *Arbor* but many, many arbors. The jungle was endless, and it was not one jungle but endless jungles, all burning with bright tigers of meaning, endless tigers. . . .

Sutty finished scanning Oryen Viya's version of *The Arbor* into her noter, put the crystal away, knocked her inner pedant on the head, and started all over.

Whatever it was she was trying to learn, the education she was trying to get, was not a religion with a creed and a sacred book. It did not deal in belief. All its books were sacred. It could not be defined by symbols and ideas, no matter how beautiful, rich, and interesting its symbols and ideas. And it was not called the Forest, though sometimes it was, or the Mountain, though sometimes it was, but was mostly, as far as she could see, called the Telling. Why?

Well (said common sense, rudely), because what the educated people *do* all the time is tell stories.

Yes, of course (her intellect replied with some disdain) they tell parables, stories, that's how they *educate*. But what do they *do?*

She set out to observe the maz.

Back on Terra, when she first studied the languages of Aka, she had learned that all the major ones had a peculiar singular/dual pronoun, used for a pregnant woman or animal and for a married couple. She had met it again in *The Arbor* and many other texts, where it referred to the single/double trunk of the tree of being and also to the mythic-heroic figures of the stories and epics, who usually—like the producer-consumer heroes of Corporation propaganda—came in pairs. This pronoun had been banned by the Corporation. Use of it in speech or writing was punishable by fine. She had never heard it spoken in Dovza City. But here she heard it daily, though not publicly, spoken of and to the teacher-officiants, the maz. Why?

Because the maz were couples. They were always couples. A sexual partnership, heterosexual or homosexual, monogamous, lifelong. More than lifelong, for if widowed they never remarried. They took and kept each other's name. The Fertiliser's wife, Ang Sotyu, had been dead fifteen years, but he was still Sotyu Ang. They were two who were one, one who was two.

Why?

She got excited. She was on the track of the central principle of the system: it was the Two that are One. She must concentrate upon understanding it.

Obliging maz gave her many texts, all more or less relevant. She learned that from the interplay of the Two arise the triple Branches that join to make the Foliages, consisting of the Four Actions and the Five Elements, to which the cosmology and the medical and ethical systems constantly referred, and which were built into the architecture and were structural to the language, particularly in its ideogrammatic form. . . . She realised that she was getting into another jungle, a very ancient one, an appallingly exuberant one. She stood on the outskirts and peered in, yearning but cautious, with conscience whining behind her like a dog. Good dog, dharma dog. She did not go into that jungle.

She remembered that she had intended to find what it was that the maz actually did.

They performed, or enacted, or did, the Telling. They told.

Some people had only a little to tell. They owned a book or poem or map or treatise that they had inherited or been given, and that, at least once a year, generally in the winter, they displayed or read aloud or recited from memory to anybody who wanted to come. Such people were politely called educated people, and were respected for owning and sharing their treasure, but they were not maz.

The maz were professionals. They gave a major part of their life to acquiring and sharing what they told, and made their living by doing so.

Some of them, specialists in ceremonies, resembled the priests of conventional Terran religions, officiating at the rites of passage, marriages, funerals, welcoming the newborn into the community, celebrating the fifteenth birthday, which was considered an important and fortunate occasion (One plus Two plus Three plus Four plus Five). The tellings of such maz were mostly formulaic—chants and rituals and recitations of the most familiar hero tales.

Some maz were physicians, healers, herbalists, or botanists. Like the leaders of exercise and gymnastic arts, they told the body, and also listened to the body (the body that was the Tree, that was the Mountain). Their tellings were factual, descriptive, medical teachings.

Some maz worked mostly with books: they taught children and adults to write and read the ideograms, they taught the texts and ways of understanding them.

But the essential work of the maz, what gave them honor among the people, was telling: reading aloud, reciting, telling stories, and talking about the stories. The more they told, the more they were honored, and the better they told it, the better they were paid. What they talked about depended on what they knew, what they possessed of the lore, what they invented on their own, and, evidently, what they felt like talking about at the moment.

The incoherence of it all was staggering. During the weeks that Sutty had laboriously learned about the Two and the One, the Tree and the Foliage, she had gone every evening to hear Maz Ottiar Uming tell a long mythico-historical saga about the explorations of the Rumay among the Eastern Isles six or seven thousand years ago, and also gone several mornings a week to hear Maz Imyen Katyan tell the origins and history of the cosmos, name the stars and constellations, and describe the movements of the other four planets in the Akan system, while displaying beautiful, accurate, ancient charts of the sky. How did it all hang together? Was there any relation at all among these disparate things?

Fed up with the abstractions of philosophy, for which she had little gift and less inclination, Sutty turned to what the maz called body-telling. The healer maz seemed to know a good deal about maintaining health. She asked Sotyu Ang to teach her about medicine. He patiently began to tell her the curative properties of each of the items in the immense herbary he had inherited from Ang Sotyu's parents, which filled most of the little drawers in his shop.

He was very pleased that she was recording all he told her in her noter. So far she had met no arcane wisdoms in the Telling, no holy secrets that could be told only to adepts, no knowledge withheld to fortify the authority of the learned, magnify their sanctity, or increase their fees. "Write down what I tell you!" all the maz kept saying. "Memorise it! Keep it to tell other people!" Sotyu Ang had spent his adult life learning the properties of the herbs, and having no disciple or apprentice, he was touchingly grateful to Sutty for preserving that knowledge. "It is all I have to give the Telling," he said. He was not a healer himself but an apothecary and herbalist. He wasn't strong on theory; his explanations of why this or that herb worked were often mere associative magic or went in pure verbal circles: this bark dispels fever because it is a febrifuge. . . . But the system of medicine that underlay this pharmaceutics was, as well as she could judge, pragmatic, preventive, and effective.

Pharmacy and medicine were one of the branches of the Great System. There were many, many branches. The endless story-telling of the maz was about many, many things. All things, all the leaves of the immense foliage of the Tree. She could not give up the conviction that there must be some guiding motive, some central concern. The trunk of the Tree. Was it ethics? the right conduct of life?

Having grown up under Unism, she was not so naive as to think there was any necessary relation between religion and morality, or that if there was a relation it was likely to be a benevolent one.

But she had begun to discern and learn a characteristic Akan ethic, expressed in all the parables and moral tales she heard in the tellings, and in the behavior and conversation of the people she knew in Okzat-Ozkat. Like the medicine, the ethic was pragmatic and preventive, and seemed to be pretty effective. It chiefly prescribed respect for your own and everybody else's body, and chiefly proscribed usury.

The frequency with which excess profit making was denounced in the stories and in public opinion showed that the root of all evil went deep on Aka. In Okzat-Ozkat, crime consisted mostly of theft, cheating, embezzlement. There was little personal violence. Assault and battery, perpetrated by thieves or by enraged victims of theft or extortion getting revenge, was so rare that every case of it was discussed for days or weeks. Crimes of passion were even rarer. They were not glamorised or condoned. In the tales and histories, heroism was not earned by murder or slaughter. Heroes were those who atoned for violent acts, or those who died bravely. The word for murderer was a cognate of the word for madman. Iziezi couldn't tell Sutty whether murderers were locked up in a jail or in a madhouse, because she didn't know of any murderers in Okzat-Ozkat. She had heard that in the old days rapists had been castrated, but wasn't sure how rape was punished now, because she didn't know of any cases of it either. Akans were gentle with their children, and Iziezi seemed to find the idea of mistreating children almost inconceivable; she knew some folktales of cruel parents, of children left orphaned who starved because nobody took them in, but she said, "Those stories are from long ago, before people were educated."

The Corporation, of course, had introduced a new ethic, with new virtues such as public spirit and patriotism, and a vast new area of crime: participation in banned activities. But Sutty had yet to meet anybody in Okzat-Ozkat, outside Corporation officials and perhaps some of the students at the Teachers' College, who thought of the maz or anything they did as criminal. Banned, illicit, illegal, deviant: these new categories redefined behavior, but they were without moral meaning except to their authors.

Had there been no crimes, then, in the old days, but rape, murder, and usury?

Maybe there had been no need for further sanctions. Maybe the system had been so universal that nobody could imagine living outside it, and only self-destructive insanity could subvert it. It had been the way of life. It had been the world.

That ubiquity of the system, its great antiquity, the tremendous force of habit it had acquired through its detailed patterning of daily life, food, drink, hours and aims of work and recreation—all this, Sutty told her noter, might explain modern Aka. At least it might explain how the Corporation of Dovza had achieved hegemony so easily, had been able to enforce uniform, minute control over how people lived, what they ate, drank, read, heard, thought, did. The system had been in place. Anciently, massively in place, all over the Continent and Isles of Aka. All Dovza had done was take the system over and change its goals. From a great consensual social pattern within which each individual sought physical and spiritual satisfaction, they had made it a great hierarchy in which each individual served the indefinite growth of the society's material wealth and complexity. From an active homeostatic balance they had turned it to an active forward-thrusting imbalance.

The difference, Sutty told her noter, was between somebody sitting thinking after a good meal and somebody running furiously to catch the bus.

She was pleased with that image.

She looked back on her first half year on Aka with

incredulity and with pity both for herself and for the con-
sumer-producers of Dovza City. "What sacrifices these
people have made!" she told her noter. "They agreed to deny
their entire culture and impoverish their lives for the 'March
to the Stars'—an artificial, theoretical goal—an imitation of
societies they assumed to be superior merely because they
were capable of space flight. Why? There's a step missing.
Something happened to cause or catalyse this enormous
change. Was it nothing more than the arrival of the First
Observers from the Ekumen? Of course that was an enormous event for a people who'd never known outsiders. . . ."

An enormous burden of responsibility on the outsiders,
too, she thought.

"Do not betray us!" the Monitor had said. But her
people, the starfarers of the Ekumen, the Observers who
were so careful not to intervene, not to interfere, not to take
control, had brought betrayal with them. A few Spaniards
arrive, and the great empires of the Incas, the Aztecs, betray
themselves, collapse, let their gods and their very language be
denied. . . . So the Akans had been their own conquerors.
Bewildered by foreign concepts, by the very concept of foreignness, they had let the ideologues of Dovza dominate and
impoverish them. As the ideologues of Communocapitalism
in the twentieth century, and the zealots of Unism in her
own century, had dominated and impoverished the Earth.

If indeed this process had begun with first contact, perhaps it was by way of reparation that Tong Ov wanted to learn

what could be learned of Aka before the First Observers
came. Did he have some hope of eventually restoring to the
Akans what they had thrown away? But the Corporation State
would never allow it. "Look in the garbage for the gold
piece," was a saying she had learned from Maz Ottiar Uming,
but she didn't think the Monitor would agree with it. To him
the gold piece was a rotten corpse.

She had mental conversations with the Monitor quite
often during that long winter of learning and listening, reading and practicing, thinking and rethinking. She set him up
as her boxing dummy. He didn't get to answer, only to listen
to her. There were things she didn't want to record in her
noter, things she thought in the privacy of her head, opinions
that she couldn't cease to cherish but tried to keep separate
from observation. Such as her opinion that if the Telling was
a religion it was very different from Terran religions, since it
entirely lacked dogmatic belief, emotional frenzy, deferral of
reward to a future life, and sanctioned bigotry. All those elements, which the Akans had done so well without, she
thought, had been introduced by Dovza. It was the Corporation State that was the religion. And so she liked to summon
up the blue-and-tan uniform, the stiff back and cold face of
the Monitor, and tell him what a zealot he was, and what a
fool, along with all the other bureaucrat-ideologues, for
grasping after other people's worthless goods while tossing his
own treasure into the garbage.

The actual flesh-and-blood Monitor must have left

Okzat-Ozkat; she had not met him in the streets for weeks. It was a relief. She much preferred him as a minatory figment.

She had stopped posing the question about what the maz did. Any four-year-old could have said what they did. They told. They retold, read, recited, discussed, explained, and invented. The infinite matter of their talk was not fixed and could not be defined. And it was still growing, even now; for not all the texts were learned from others, not all the stories were of ancient days, not all the thoughts and ideas had been handed down over the years.

The first time she met the maz Odiedin Manma was at a telling where he told the story of a young man, a villager up in the foothills of Silong, who dreamed that he could fly. The young man dreamed flying so often and so vividly that it seemed he began to take his dreams for waking life. He would describe the sensations of flight and the things he saw from the air. He drew maps of beautiful unknown lands on the other side of the world that he discovered in his flights. People came to hear him tell about flying and to see the marvelous maps. But one day, climbing down a river gorge after a strayed eberdin, he missed his footing, fell, and was killed.

That was all the story. Odiedin Manma made no comment, and no one asked questions. The telling was at the house of the maz Ottiar and Uming. Sutty later asked Maz Ottiar Uming about the story, for it puzzled her.

The old woman said, "Odiedin's partner Manma was

killed in a fall when he was twenty-seven. They had been maz only a year."

"And Manma used to tell his dreams of flying?"

Ottiar Uming shook her head. "No," she said. "That is the story, yoz. Odiedin Manma's story. He tells that one. The rest of his telling is in the body." She meant exercises, gymnastic practice, of which Odiedin was a highly respected teacher.

"I see," Sutty said, and went away and thought about it.

She knew one thing, she had learned one thing for sure, here in Okzat-Ozkat: she had learned how to listen. To listen, hear, keep listening to what she'd heard. To carry the words away and listen to them. If telling was the skill of the maz, listening was the skill of the yoz. As they all liked to remark, neither one was any use without the other.

F I V E

WINTER CAME WITHOUT much snow but bitterly cold, winds knifing down out of the immense wilderness of mountains to the west and north. Iziezi took Sutty to a secondhand clothing store to buy a worn but sturdy leather coat lined with its own silky fleece. The hood lining was the feathery fur of some mountain animal of which Iziezi said, "All gone now. Too many hunters." She said the leather was not eberdin, as Sutty had thought, but minule, from the high mountains. The coat came below her knees and was met by light, fleece-lined boots. These were new, made of artificial materials, for mountain sports and hiking. The people of the old way placidly accepted new technologies and products, so long as they worked better than the old ones and so long as using them did not require changing one's life in any important way. To Sutty this seemed a profound but reasonable conservatism. But to an economy predicated on endless growth, it was anathema.

Sutty tramped around the icy streets in her old coat and her new boots. In winter in Okzat-Ozkat everybody looked alike in their old leather coats and fleecy hoods, except for the uniformed bureaucrats, who all looked alike in their coats and hoods of artificial fabrics in bright uniform colors, purple, rust, and blue. The merciless cold gave a kind of fellowship of anonymity. When you got indoors the warmth was an unfailing source of relief, pleasure, companionly feeling. On a bitter blue evening, to struggle up the steep streets to some small, stuffy, dim-lit room and gather with the others at the hearth—an electric heater, for there was little wood here near timberline, and all warmth was generated by the ice-cold energy of the Ereha—and to take your mittens off and rub your hands, which seemed so naked and delicate, and look round at the other windburned faces and ice-dewed eyelashes, and hear the little drum go tabatt, tabatt, and the soft voice begin to speak, listing the names of the rivers of Hoying and how each flowed into the next, or telling the story of Ezid and Inamema on the Mountain of Gam, or describing how the Council of Mez raised an army against the western barbarians—that was a solid, enduring, reliable pleasure to Sutty, all winter long.

The western barbarians, she now knew, were the
Dovzans. Almost everything the maz taught, all their legends
and history and philosophy, came from the center and east of
the great continent, and from past centuries, past millennia.
Nothing came from Dovza but the language they spoke; and
here that was full of words from the original language of this
area, Rangma, and other tongues.

Words. A world made of words.

There was music. Some of the maz sang healing chants
like those Tong Ov had recorded in the city; some played
string instruments, plucked or bowed, to accompany narrative ballads and songs. Sutty recorded them when she could,
though her musical stupidity kept her from appreciating
them. There had been art, carvings and paintings and tapes-
tries, using the symbols of the Tree and the Mountain and
figures and events from the legends and histories. There had
been dance, and there were still the various forms of exercise
and moving meditation. But first and last there were the
words.

When the maz put the mantle of their office—a flimsy
length of red or blue cloth—over their shoulders, they were
perceived as owning a sacred authority or power. What they
said then was part of the Telling.

When they took the scarf off they returned to ordinary sta-
tus, claiming no personal spiritual authority at all; what they
said then weighed no more than what anybody said. Some
people of course insisted on ascribing permanent authority to

them. Like the people of Sutty's own tribe, many Akans longed to follow a leader, turn earned payment into tribute, load responsibility onto somebody else's shoulders. But if the maz had one quality in common, it was a stubborn modesty. They were not in the charisma business. Maz Imyen Katyan was as gentle a man as she had ever met, but when a woman called him by a reverent title, munan, used for famous maz in the stories and histories, he turned on her with real rage— "How dare you call me that?"—and then, having regained his calm, "When I've been dead a hundred years, yoz."

Sutty had assumed that since everything the maz did professionally was in defiance of the law, at real personal risk, some of this modest style, this very low profile, was a recent thing. But when she said so, Maz Ottiar Uming shook her head.

"Oh, no," the old woman said. "We have to hide, to keep everything secret, yes. But in my grandparents' time I think most of the maz lived the way we do. Nobody can wear the scarf all the time! Not even Maz Elyed Oni. . . . Of course it was different in the umyazu."

"Tell me about the umyazu, maz."

"They were places built so the power could gather in them. Places full of being. Full of people telling and listening. Full of books."

"Where were they?"

"Oh, everywhere. Here in Okzat-Ozkat there was one up where the High School is now, and one where the pumice works is now. And all the way to Silong, in the high valleys, on the trade roads, there were umyazu for the pilgrims. And down where the land's rich, there were huge, great umyazu, with hundreds of maz living in them, and visiting from one to another all their lives. They kept books, and wrote them, and made records, and kept on telling. They could give their whole life to it, you see. They could always be there where it was. People would go visit them to hear the telling and read the books in the libraries. People went in processions, with red and blue flags. They'd go and stay all winter, sometimes. Save up for years so they could pay the maz and pay for their lodging. My grandmother told me about going to the Red Umyazu of Tenban. She was eleven or twelve years old. It took them nearly the whole year to go and stay and come back. They were pretty wealthy, my grandmother's family, so they could ride all the way, the whole family, with eberdin pulling the wagon. They didn't have the cars and planes then, you know. Nobody did. Most people just walked. But everybody had flags and wore ribbons. Red and blue." Ottiar Uming laughed with pleasure at the thought of those processions. "My mother's mother wrote the story of that journey. I'll get it out and tell it sometime."

Her partner, Uming Ottiar, was unfolding a big, stiff square of paper on the table in the back room of their grocery shop. Ottiar Uming went to help him, setting a polished black stone on each curling corner to keep it flat. Then they

invited their five listeners to come forward, salute the paper
with the mountain-heart gesture, and study the chart and
inscriptions on it. They displayed it thus every three weeks,
and Sutty had come each time all winter. It had been her first
formal introduction to the thought system of the Tree. The
couple's most precious possession, given them fifty years ago
by their teacher-maz, it was a marvelously painted map or
mandala of the One that is Two giving rise to the Three, to
the Five, to the Myriad, and the Myriad again to the Five, the
Three, the Two, the One. . . . A Tree, a Body, a Mountain,
inscribed within the circle that was everything and nothing.
Delicate little figures, animals, people, plants, rocks, rivers,
lively as flickering flames, made up each of the greater forms,
which divided, rejoined, transformed each into the others
and into the whole, the unity made up of infinite variety, the
mystery plain as day.

Sutty loved to study it and try to make out the inscriptions and poems surrounding it. The painting was beautiful,
the poetry was splendid and elusive, the whole chart was a
work of high art, absorbing, enlightening. Maz Uming sat
down and after a few knocks on his drum began intoning one
of the interminable chants that accompanied the rituals and
many of the tellings. Maz Ottiar read and discussed some of
the inscriptions, which were four or five hundred years old.
Her voice was soft, full of silences. Softly and hesitantly, the
students asked questions. She answered them the same way.

Then she drew back and sat down and took up the chant in a gnat voice, and old Uming, half blind, his speech thickened by a stroke, got up and talked about one of the poems.

"That's by Maz Niniu Raying, five, six, seven hundred years back, eh? It's in *The Arbor*. Somebody wrote it here, a good calligrapher, because it talks about how the leaves of the Tree perish but always return so long as we see them and say them. See, here it says: 'Word, the gold beyond the fall, returns the glory to the branch.' And underneath it here, see, somebody later on wrote, 'Mind's life is memory.'" He smiled round at them, a kind, lopsided smile. "Remember that, eh? 'Mind's life is memory.' Don't forget!" He laughed, they laughed. All the while, out front in the grocery shop, the maz' grandson kept the volume turned up high on the audio system, cheery music, exhortations, and news announcements blaring out to cover the illicit poetry, the forbidden laughter.

It was a pity, but no surprise, Sutty told her noter, that an ancient popular cosmology-philosophy-spiritual discipline should contain a large proportion of superstition and verge over into what she labeled in her noter HP, hocus-pocus. The great jungle of significance had its swamps and morasses, and she had at last stumbled into some of them. She met a few maz who claimed arcane knowledge and supernal powers. Boring as she found all such claims, she knew she could not be sure of what was valuable and what was drivel, and painstakingly recorded whatever information she could buy from these maz concerning alchemy, numerology, and literal readings of symbolic texts. They sold her bits of texts and snippets of methodology at a fairly stiff price, grudgingly, hedging the transactions with portentous warnings about the danger of this powerful knowledge.

She particularly detested the literal readings. By such literalism, fundamentalism, religions betrayed the best intentions of their founders. Reducing thought to formula, replacing choice by obedience, these preachers turned the living word into dead law. But she put it all into her noter— which she had now had to unload into crystal storage twice, for she could not transmit any of the treasure-and-trash she was amassing.

At this distance, with all means of communication monitored, there was no way to consult with Tong Ov as to what she should or he intended to do with all this material. She couldn't even tell him she'd found it. The problem remained, and grew.

Among the HP she came on a brand that was, as far as she knew, unique to Aka: a system of arcane significances attached to the various strokes that composed the ideogrammatic characters and the further strokes and dots that qualified them with verbal tense and mode and nominal case and with Action or Element (for everything, literally every thing, could be categorised under the Four Actions and the Five Elements). Every character of the old writing thus became a code to be interpreted by specialists, who functioned much

as horoscope readers had in Sutty's homeland. She discovered that many people in Okzat-Ozkat, including officials of
the Corporation, would undertake nothing of importance
without calling in a 'sign reader' to write out their name and
other relevant words and, after poring over these and refer-
ring to impressively elaborate charts and diagrams, to advise
and foretell. "This is the kind of thing that makes me sympa-
thise with the Monitor," she told her noter. Then she said,
"No. It's what the Monitor wants from his own kind of HP.
Political HP. Everything locked in place, on course, under
control. But he's handed over the controls just as much as
they have."

Many of the practices she learned about had equivalents
on Earth. The exercises, like yoga and tai chi, were physical-
mental, a lifelong discipline, leading toward mindfulness, or
toward a trance state, or toward martial vigor and readiness,
depending on the style and the practitioner's desire. Trance
seemed to be sought for its own sake as an experience of
essential stillness and balance rather than as satori or revela-
tion. Prayer . . . Well, what about prayer?

The Akans did not pray.

That seemed so strange, so unnatural, that as soon as she
had the thought, she qualified it: it was very possible that she
didn't properly understand what prayer was.

If it meant asking for something, they didn't do it. Not
even to the extent that she did. She knew that when she was
very startled she cried, "O Ram!" and when she was very

frightened she whispered, "O please, please." The words
were strictly meaningless, yet she knew they were a kind of
prayer. She had never heard an Akan say anything of the
kind. They could wish one another well—"May you have a
good year, may your venture prosper"—just as they could
curse one another—"May your sons eat stones," she had
heard Diodi the barrow man murmur as a blue-and-tan
stalked by. But those were wishes, not prayers. People didn't
ask God to make them good or to destroy their enemy. They
didn't ask the gods to win them the lottery or cure their sick
child. They didn't ask the clouds to let the rain fall or the
grain grow. They wished, they willed, they hoped, but they
didn't pray.

If prayer was praise, then perhaps they did pray. She had
come to understand their descriptions of natural phenomena,
the Fertiliser's pharmacopoeia, the maps of the stars, the lists
of ores and minerals, as litanies of praise. By naming the names
they rejoiced in the complexity and specificity, the wealth
and beauty of the world, they participated in the fullness of
being. They described, they named, they told all about everything. But they did not pray for anything.

Nor did they sacrifice anything. Except money.

To get money, you had to give money: that was a firm and
universal principle. Before any business undertaking, they
buried silver and brass coins, or threw them into the river, or
gave them to beggars. They pounded out gold coins into airy,
translucent gold leaf with which they decorated niches,

columns, even whole walls of buildings, or had them spun
into thread and woven into gorgeous shawls and scarves to
give away on New Year's Day. Silver and gold coins were hard
to come by, as the Corporation, detesting this extravagant
waste, had gone over mostly to paper; so people burned paper
money like incense, made paper boats of it and sailed them
off on the river, chopped it up fine and ate it with salad. The
practice was pure HP, but Sutty found it irresistible. Slaugh-
tering goats or one's firstborn to placate the supernatural
seemed to her the worst kind of perversity, but she saw a gam-
bler's gallantry in this money sacrifice. Easy come, easy go. At
the New Year, when you met a friend or acquaintance, you
each lighted a one-ha bill and waved it about like a little
torch, wishing each other health and prosperity. She saw
even employees of the Corporation doing this. She wondered
if the Monitor had ever done it.

The more naive people that she came to know at the
tellings and in the classes, and Diodi and other friendly
acquaintances of the streets, all believed in sign reading and
alchemical marvels and talked about diets that let you live
forever, exercises that had given the ancient heroes the
strength to withstand whole armies. Even Iziezi held firmly
by sign reading. But most of the maz, the educated, the
teachers, claimed no special powers or attainments at all.
They lived firmly and wholly in the real world. Spiritual
yearning and the sense of sacredness they knew, but they did
not know anything holier than the world, they did not seek a

power greater than nature. Sutty was certain of that. *No miracles!* she told her noter, jubilant.

She coded her notes, got into her coat and boots, and set off through the vicious early-spring wind for Maz Odiedin Manma's exercise class. Silong was visible for the first time in weeks, not the barrier wall but only the peak above it, standing like a silver horn over dark storm clouds.

She went regularly to exercise with Iziezi now, often staying on to watch Akidan and other adolescents and young people do "two-one," an athletic form performed in pairs, with spectacular feints and falls. Odiedin Manma, the teller of the strange story about the man who dreamed he could fly, was much admired by these young people, and some of them had first taken Sutty to his class. He taught an austere, very beautiful form of exercise-meditation. He had invited her to join his group.

They met in an old warehouse down by the river, a less safe place than the umyazu-turned-gymnasium she went to with Iziezi, where legitimate health-manual gymnastics did take place and served as cover for the illegal ones. The warehouse was lighted only by dirty slit windows high up under the eaves. Nobody spoke above the barest whisper. There was no hocus-pocus about Odiedin, but Sutty found the class, the silent, slow movements in darkness, hauntingly strange, sometimes disturbing; it had entered into her dreams.

A man sitting near Sutty this morning stared at her as she took her place on the mat. While the group went through the first part of the form, he kept staring, winking, gesturing, grinning at her. Nobody behaved like that. She was annoyed and embarrassed until, during a long-held pose, she got a look at the man and realised that he was half-witted.

When the group began a set of movements she wasn't yet familiar with, she watched and followed along as best she could. Her mistakes and omissions upset her neighbor. He kept trying to show her when and how to move, pantomiming, exaggerating gestures. When they stood up, she stayed sitting, which was always permissible, but this distressed the poor fellow very much. He gestured, Up! up! He mouthed the word, and pointed upward. Finally, whispering, "Up— like this—see?," he took a step onto the air. He brought the other foot up on the invisible stair, and then climbed another step up the same way. He was standing barefoot half a meter above the floor, looking down at her, smiling anxiously and gesturing for her to join him. He was standing on the air.

Odiedin, a lithe, trim man of fifty with a scrap of blue cloth around his neck, came to him. All the others kept on steadily with the complex, swaying kelp-forest patterns. Odiedin murmured, "Come down, Uki." Reaching up, he took the man's hand and led him down two nonexistent steps to the floor, patted his shoulder gently, and moved on. Uki joined in the pattern, swaying and turning with flawless grace and power. He had evidently forgotten Sutty.

She could not bring herself to ask Odiedin any questions

after the class. What would she ask? "Did you see what I saw? Did I?" That would be stupid. It couldn't have happened, and so he'd no doubt merely answer her question with a question.

Or perhaps the reason she didn't ask was that she was afraid he would simply answer, "Yes."

If a mime can make air into a box, if a fakir can climb a rope tied to air, maybe a poor fool can make air into a step. If spiritual strength can move mountains, maybe it can make stairs. Trance state. Hypnotic or hypnogogic suggestion.

She described the occurrence briefly in her daily notes, without comment. As she spoke into her noter, she became quite sure that there had in fact been some kind of step there that she hadn't seen in the dim light, a block, a box perhaps, painted black. Of course there had been something there. She paused, but did not say anything more. She could see the block or box, now. But she had not seen it.

But often in her mind's eye she saw those two callused, muscular, bare feet stepping up the absent mountain. She wondered what the air felt like on the soles of your feet when you walked on it. Cool? Resilient?

After that she made herself pay more attention to the old texts and tales that talked about walking on the wind, riding on clouds, traveling to the stars, destroying distant enemies with thunderbolts. Such feats were always ascribed to heroes and wise maz far away and long ago, even though a good many of them had been made commonplace fact by modern technologies. She still thought they were mythic, metaphoric, not meant to be taken literally. She arrived at no explanation.

But her attitude had been changed. She knew now that she'd still missed the point, a misunderstanding so gross and total that she couldn't see it.

A telling is not an explaining.

Can't see the forest for the trees, the pedants, the pundits, Uncle Hurree growled in her mind. *Poetry, girl, poetry. Read the Mahabharata. Everything's there.*

"Maz Elyed," she asked, "what is it you do?"

"I tell, yoz Sutty."

"Yes. But the stories, all the things you tell, what do they do?"

"They tell the world."

"Why, maz?"

"That's what people do, yoz. What we're here for."

Maz Elyed, like many of the maz, talked softly and rather hesitantly, pausing, starting up again about the time you thought she'd stopped. Silence was part of all she said.

She was small, lame, and very wrinkled. Her family owned a little hardware shop in the poorest district of the city, where many houses were not built of stone and wood but were tents or yurts of felt and canvas patched with plastic, set on platforms of beaten clay. Nephews and grandnieces abounded in the hardware shop. A very small great-grandnephew staggered about it, his goal in life to eat screws and washers. An old 2D photograph of Elyed with her partner Oni hung on the wall behind the counter: Oni Elyed tall and dreamy-eyed, Elyed Oni tiny, vivid, beautiful. Thirty years ago they had been arrested for sexual deviance and teaching rotten-corpse ideology. They were sent to a re-education camp on the west coast. Oni had died there. Elyed came back after ten years, lame, with no teeth: knocked out or lost to scurvy, she never said. She did not talk about herself or her wife or her age or her concerns. Her days were spent in an unbroken ritual continuity that included all bodily needs and functions, preparing and eating meals, sleeping, teaching, but above all reading and telling, a soft, endless repetition of the texts she had been learning her whole life long.

At first Elyed had appeared unearthly, inhuman to Sutty, as indifferent and inaccessible as a cloud, a domestic saint living entirely inside the ritual system, a sort of automaton of recitation without emotion or personality. Sutty had feared her. She was afraid that this woman who embodied the system fully, who lived it totally, would force her to admit that it was hysterical, obsessional, absolutist, everything she hated and feared and wanted it not to be. But as she listened to Elyed's tellings, she heard a disciplined, reasoning mind, though it spoke of what was unreasonable.

Elyed used that word often, unreasonable, in a literal sense: what cannot be understood by thinking. Once when

Sutty was trying to find a coherent line of thought connecting several different tellings, Elyed said, "What we do is unreasonable, yoz."

"But there is a reason *for* it."

"Probably."

"What I don't understand is the pattern. The place, the importance of things in the pattern. Yesterday you were telling the story about Iaman and Deberren, but you didn't finish it, and today you read the descriptions of the leaves of the trees of the grove at the Golden Mountain. I don't understand what they have to do with each other. Or is it that on certain days a certain kind of material is proper? Or are my questions just stupid?"

"No," the maz said, and laughed her small laugh that had no teeth to show. "I get tired remembering. So I read. It doesn't matter. It's all the leaves of the tree."

"So . . . anything—anything that's in the books is equally important?"

Elyed considered. "No," she said. "Yes." She drew a shaky breath. She tired quickly when she could not rest in the stream of ritual act and language, but she never dismissed Sutty, never evaded her questions. "It's all we have. You see? It's the way we have the world. Without the telling, we don't have anything at all. The moment goes by like the water of the river. We'd tumble and spin and be helpless if we tried to live in the moment. We'd be like a baby. A baby can do it, but we'd drown. Our minds need to tell, need the telling. To hold. The past has passed, and there's nothing in the future to catch hold of. The future is nothing yet. How could anybody live there? So what we have is the words that tell what happened and what happens. What was and is."

"Memory?" Sutty said. "History?"

Elyed nodded, dubious, not satisfied by these terms. She sat thinking for some time and finally said, "We're not outside the world, yoz. You know? We are the world. We're its language. So we live and it lives. You see? If we don't say the words, what is there in our world?"

She was trembling, little spasms of the hands and mouth that she tried to conceal. Sutty thanked her with the mountain-heart gesture, apologised for wearing her out with talk. Elyed gave her small, black laugh. "Oh, yoz, I keep going with talk. Just the way the world does," she said.

Sutty went away and brooded. All this about language. It always came back to words. Like the Greeks with their Logos, the Hebrew Word that was God. But this was words. Not the Logos, the Word, but words. Not one but many, many. . . . Nobody made the world, ruled the world, told the world to be. It was. It did. And human beings made it be, made it be a human world, by saying it? By telling what was in it and what happened in it? Anything, everything—tales of heroes, maps of the stars, love songs, lists of the shapes of leaves. . . . For a moment she thought she understood.

She brought this half-formed understanding to Maz Ottiar Uming, who was easier to talk with than Elyed, want-

ing to try to put it into words. But Ottiar was busy with a
chant, so Sutty talked to Uming, and somehow her words got
contorted and pedantic. She couldn't speak her intuition.

As they struggled to understand each other, Uming Ottiar
showed a bitterness, almost the first Sutty had met with among
these soft-voiced teachers. Despite his impediment he was a
fluent talker, and he got going, mildly enough at first: "Animals
have no language. They have their nature. You see? They
know the way, they know where to go and how to go, following
their nature. But we're animals with no nature. Eh? Animals
with no nature! That's strange! We're so strange! We have to
talk about how to go and what to do, think about it, study it,
learn it. Eh? We're born to be reasonable, so we're born ignorant. You see? If nobody teaches us the words, the thoughts, we
stay ignorant. If nobody shows a little child, two, three years
old, how to look for the way, the signs of the path, the landmarks, then it gets lost on the mountain, doesn't it? And dies in
the night, in the cold. So. So." He rocked his body a little.

Maz Ottiar, across the little room, knocked on the drum,
murmuring some long chronicle of ancient days to a single,
sleepy, ten-year-old listener.

Maz Uming rocked and frowned. "So, without the
telling, the rocks and plants and animals go on all right. But
the people don't. People wander around. They don't know a
mountain from its reflection in a puddle. They don't know a
path from a cliff. They hurt themselves. They get angry and
hurt each other and the other things. They hurt animals

because they're angry. They make quarrels and cheat each other. They want too much. They neglect things. Crops don't get planted. Too many crops get planted. Rivers get dirty with shit. Earth gets dirty with poison. People eat poison food. Everything is confused. Everybody's sick. Nobody looks after the sick people, the sick things. But that's very bad, very bad, eh? Because looking after things, that's our job, eh? Looking after things, looking after each other. Who else would do it? Trees? Rivers? Animals? They just do what they are. But we're here, and we have to learn how to be here, how to do things, how to keep things going the way they need to go. The rest of the world knows its business. Knows the One and the Myriad, the Tree and the Leaves. But all we know is how to learn. How to study, how to listen, how to talk, how to tell. If we don't tell the world, we don't know the world. We're lost in it, we die. But we have to tell it right, tell it truly. Eh? Take care and tell it truly. That's what went wrong. Down there, down there in Dovza, when they started telling lies. Those false maz, those big munan, those boss maz. Telling people that nobody knew the truth but them, nobody could speak but them, everybody had to tell the same lies they told. Traitors, usurers! Leading people astray for money! Getting rich off their lies, bossing people! No wonder the world stopped going around! No wonder the police took over!"

The old man was dark red in the face, shaking his good hand as if he held a stick in it. His wife got up, came over, and put the drum and drumstick into his hands, all the time going on with her droning recitation. Uming bit his lip, shook his head, fretted a bit, knocked the drum rather hard, and took up the recitation on the next line.

"I'm sorry," Sutty said to Ottiar as the old woman went with her to the door. "I didn't mean to upset Maz Uming."

"Oh, it's all right," Ottiar said. "All that was before I/we were born. Down in Dovza."

"You weren't part of Dovza, up here?"

"We're mostly Rangma here. My/our people all talked Rangma. The grandparents didn't know how to talk much Dovzan till after the Corporation police came and made everybody talk it. They hated it! They kept the worst accents they could!"

She had a merry smile, and Sutty smiled back; but she walked down the hill-street in a maze of thoughts. Uming's tirade against the 'boss maz' had been about the period *before* the Dovzan Corporation ruled the world, before 'the police came,' possibly before the First Observers of the Ekumen came. As he spoke, it had occurred to her that of the hundreds of stories and histories she had heard in the tellings, none had to do with events in Dovza, or any events of the last five or six decades except very local ones. She had never heard a maz tell a tale about the coming of the offworlders, the rise of the Corporation State, or any public event of the last seventy years or more.

"Iziezi," she said that night, "who were the boss maz?"

She was helping Iziezi peel a kind of fungus that had just

come into season up on the hills where the snow was melting at the edge of thawing drifts. It was called demyedi, first-of-spring, tasted like snow, and was good for balancing the pep-pery banam shoots and the richness of oilfish, thus keeping the sap thin and the heart easy. Whatever else she had missed and misunderstood in this world, she had learned when, and why, and how to cook its food.

"Oh, that was a long time ago," said Iziezi. "When they started bossing everybody around, down in Dovza."

"A hundred years ago?"

"Maybe that long ago."

"Who are 'the police'?"

"Oh, you know. The blue-and-tans."

"Just them?"

"Well, I guess we call all those people the police. From down there. Dovzans. . . . First they used to arrest the boss maz. Then they started to arrest all the maz. When they sent soldiers up here to arrest people in the umyazu, that's when people started calling them police. And people call skuyen the police, too. Or they say, 'They're working for the police.'"

"Skuyen?"

"People who tell the blue-and-tans about illegal things. Books, tellings, anything. . . . For money. Or for hatred." Iziezi's mild voice changed on the last words. Her face had closed into its tight look of pain.

Books, tellings, anything. What you cooked. Who you made love with. How you wrote the word for tree. Anything.

No wonder the system was incoherent, fragmented. No wonder Uming's world had stopped going around. The wonder was that anything remained of it at all.

As if her realisations had summoned him out of nothingness, the Monitor passed her on the street next morning. He did not look at her.

A few days later she went to visit Maz Sotyu Ang. His shop was closed. It had never been closed before. She asked a neighbor sweeping his front step if he would be back soon. "I think the producer-consumer is away," the man said vaguely.

Maz Elyed had lent her a beautiful old book—lent or given, she was not sure. "Keep it, it's safe with you," Elyed had said. It was an ancient anthology of poems from the Eastern Isles, an inexhaustible treasure. She was deep in studying and transferring it into her noter. Several days passed before she thought to visit her old friend the Fertiliser again. She walked up the steep street that shone blinding black in the sunshine. Spring came late but fast to these foothills of the great range. The air blazed with light. She walked past the shop without recognising it.

She was disoriented, turned back, found the shop. It was all white: whitewashed, a blank front. All the signs, the bold characters, the old words gone. Silenced. Snowfall. . . . The door stood ajar. She looked in. The counters and the walls of tiny drawers had been torn out. The room was empty, dirty, ransacked. The walls where she had seen the living words, the breathing words, had been smeared over with brown paint.

The twice-forked lightning tree. . . .

The neighbor had come out when she passed. He was sweeping his step again. She began to speak to him and then did not. Skuyen? How did you know?

She started back home and then, seeing the river glittering at the foot of the streets, turned and went along the hillside out of town to a path that led down to and followed the river. She had hiked that path all one day, one of those days long, long ago in the early autumn when she was waiting for the Envoy to tell her to go back to the city.

She set off upriver beside thickets of newly leafed-out shrubs and the dwarfed trees that grew here not far from timberline. The Ereha ran milky blue with the first glacier melt. Ice crunched in the ruts of the road, but the sun was hot on her head and back. Her mouth was still dry with shock. Her throat ached.

Go back to the city. She should go back to the city. Now. With the three record crystals and the noter full of stuff, full of poetry. Get it all to Tong Ov before the Monitor got it.

There was no way to send it. She must take it. But travel must be authorised. O Ram! where was her ZIL? She hadn't worn it for months. Nobody here used ZILs, only if you worked for the Corporation or had to go to one of the bureaus. It was in her briefcase, in her room. She'd have to use her ZIL at the telephone on Dock Street, get through to Tong, ask him to get her an authorisation to come to the city. By plane. Take the riverboat down to Eltli and fly from there.

Do it all out in the open, let them all know, so they couldn't stop her privately, trick her somehow. Confiscate her records. Silence her. Where was Maz Sotyu? What were they doing to him? Was it her fault?

She could not think about that now. What she had to do was save what she could of what Sotyu had given her. Sotyu and Ottiar and Uming and Odiedin and Elyed and Iziezi, dear Iziezi. She could not think about that now.

She turned round, walked hurriedly back along the river into town, found her ZIL bracelet in her briefcase in her room, went to Dock Street, and put in a call to Tong Ov at the Ekumenical Office in Dovza City.

His Dovzan secretary answered and said superciliously that he was in a meeting. "I must speak to him, now," Sutty said and was not surprised when the secretary said in a meek tone that she would call him.

When Sutty heard his voice she said, in Hainish, hearing the words as foreign and strange, "Envoy, I've been out of touch for so long, I feel as if we needed to talk."

"I see," Tong said, and a few other meaningless things, while she and probably he tried to figure out how to say anything meaningful. If only he knew any of her languages, if only she knew his! But their only common languages were Hainish and Dovzan.

"Nothing devolving in particular?" he inquired.

"No, no, not really. But I'd like to bring you the material

I've been collecting," she said. "Just notes on daily life in Okzat-Ozkat."

"I was hoping to come see you there, but that seems to be contraindicated at present," Tong said. "With a window just wide enough for one, of course it's a pity to close the blinds. But I know how much you love Dovza City and must have been missing it. I'm equally sure that you've found nothing much interesting up there. So, if your work's all done, by all means come on back and enjoy yourself here."

Sutty groped and stammered, and finally said, "Well, as you know it's a very, the Corporation State is a very homogeneous culture, very powerful and definitely in control, very successful. So everything here is, yes, is very much the same here as there. But maybe I should stay on and finish the, finish the tapes before I bring them? They're not very interesting."

"Here, as you know," said Tong, "our hosts share all kinds of information with us. And we share ours with them. Everybody here is getting loads of fresh material, very educational and inspiring. So what you're doing there isn't really all that important. Don't worry about it. Of course I'm not at all uneasy about you. And have no need to be. Do I?"

"No, yes, of course not," she said. "Honestly."

She left the telephone office, showing her ZIL at the door, and hurried back to her inn, her home. She thought she had followed Tong's backward talk, but it destroyed itself in her memory. She thought he had been trying to tell her to stay there, not to try to bring what she had to him, because he would have to show it to officials there and it would be confiscated, but she was not sure that was what he had meant. Maybe he truly meant it was not all that important. Maybe he meant he could not help her at all.

Helping Iziezi prepare dinner, she was sure that she had panicked, had been stupid to call Tong, thus bringing attention to herself and her friends and informants here. Feeling that she must be careful, cautious, she said nothing about the desecrated shop.

Iziezi had known Maz Sotyu Ang for years, but she said nothing about him either. She showed no sign of anything being wrong. She showed Sutty how to slice the fresh numiem, thin and on the bias, to bring the flavor out.

It was one of Elyed's teaching nights. After she and Akidan and Iziezi had eaten, Sutty took her leave and went down River Street into the poor part of town, the yurt city, where the Corporation had not brought electric enlightenment and there were only the tiny gleams of oil lamps inside the shacks and tents. It was cold, but not the bone-dry, blade-keen cold of winter. A damp, spring-smelling cold, full of life. But Sutty's heart swelled with dread as she came near Elyed's shop: to find it all whited out, gutted, raped . . .

The great-grandnephew was screaming bloody murder as somebody separated him from a screwdriver, and nieces smiled at Sutty as she went through the shop to the back room. She was early for the teaching hour. Nobody was in the little room but the maz and an unobtrusive grandnephew setting up chairs.

"Maz Elyed Oni, do you know Maz Sotyu Ang—the herbalist—his shop—" She could not keep the words from bursting out.

"Yes," the old woman said. "He's staying with his daughter."

"The shop, the herbary—"

"That is gone."

"But—"

Her throat ached. She struggled with tears of rage and outrage that wanted to be cried, here with this woman who could be her grandmother, who was her grandmother.

"It was my fault."

"No," Elyed said. "You did no wrong. Sotyu Ang did no wrong. There is no fault. Things are going badly. It's not possible always to do right when things are difficult."

Sutty stood silent. She looked around the small, high-ceilinged room, its red rug almost hidden by chairs and cushions; everything poor, clean; a bunch of paper flowers stuck in an ugly vase on the low table; the grandnephew gently rearranging floor cushions; the old, old woman lowering herself carefully, painfully onto a thin pillow near the table. On the table, a book. Old, worn, many times read.

"I think maybe, yoz Sutty, it was the other way round. Sotyu told us last summer that he thought a neighbor had informed the police about his herbary. Then you came, and nothing happened."

Sutty forced herself to understand what Elyed had said. "I was a safeguard?"

"I think so."

"Because they don't want me to see . . . what they do? But then why did they—now—?"

Elyed drew her thin shoulders together. "They don't study patience," she said.

"Then I should stay here," Sutty said slowly, trying to understand. "I thought it would be better for you if I left."

"I think you might go to Silong."

Her mind was clouded. "To Silong?"

"The last umyazu is there."

Sutty said nothing, and after a while Elyed added, scrupulous of fact, "The last I know of. Maybe some are left in the east, in the Isles. But here in the west they say the Lap of Silong is the last. Many, many books have been sent there. For many years now. It must be a great library. Not like the Golden Mountain, not like the Red Umyazu, not like Atangen. But what has been saved, most of it is there."

She looked at Sutty, her head a little on one side, a small old bird, keen-eyed. She had completed her cautious journey down onto the cushion, and now arranged her black wool vest, a bird getting its feathers straight. "You want to learn the Telling, I know that. You should go there," she said. "Here, nothing much is here. Bits and pieces. What I have, what a few maz have. Not much. Always less. Go to Silong, daughter Sutty. Maybe you can find a partner. Be a maz. Eh?" Her face creased up in a sudden, tremendous smile, toothless and radiant. She jiggled gently with laughter. "Go to Silong . . ."

Other people were coming in. Elyed put her hands in her lap and began to chant softly, "The two from one, the one from two. . . ."

SIX

SHE WENT TO talk to Odiedin Manma. Despite his enigmatic telling, despite the uncanny event (which she was now quite sure she had merely imagined) in his class, she had found him the most worldly and politically knowledgeable of the maz she knew, and she badly wanted some practical counsel. She waited till after his class and then begged him for advice.

"Does Maz Elyed want me to go to this place, this umyazu, because she thinks if I go there, my presence will help keep it safe? I think she might be wrong. I think the blue-and-tans are tracking me all the time. It's a secret place, a hidden place, isn't it? If I went, they could just follow me. They may have all kinds of tracking devices."

Odiedin held up his hand, mild but unsmiling. "I don't think they'll track you, yoz. They have orders from Dovza to let you be. Not to follow and observe you."

"You know that?"

He nodded.

She believed him. She remembered the invisible web she had sensed when she first lived here. Odiedin was one of the spiders.

"Anyhow, the way to Silong isn't an easy track to follow. And you could leave very quietly." He chewed his lip a little. A hint of warmth, a pleasurable look, had come into his dark, severe face. "If Maz Elyed suggested that you go there, and if you want to go there," he said, "I'd show you the way."

"You would?"

"I was at the Lap of Silong once. I was twelve. My parents were maz. It was a bad time then. When the books were burned. A lot of police. A lot of loss, destruction, Arrests. Fear. So we left Okzat, went up into the hills, to the hill towns. And then, in the summer, all the way round Zubuam, to the lap of the Mother. I'd like very much to go that way again before I die, yoz."

————

Sutty tried to leave no track, 'no footprints in the dust.' She sent no word to Tong except that she planned to do nothing much the next few months except a little hiking and climb-

ing. She spoke to none of her friends, acquaintances, teachers, except Elyed and Odiedin. She fretted about her crystals—four, now, for she had cleared her noter again. She
could not leave them at Iziezi's house, the first place the
blue-and-tans would look for them. She was trying to decide
where to bury them and how to do it without being seen,
when Ottiar and Uming in the most casual way told her that
since the police were so busy at the moment, they were stor-
ing their mandala away in a safe place for a while, and did
she have anything she'd like to stash away with it? Their intuition seemed amazing, until Sutty remembered that they
were part of the spiderweb—and had lived their adult lives in
secrecy, hiding all that was most precious to them. She gave
them the crystals. They told her where the hiding place was.
"Just in case," Ottiar said mildly. She told them who Tong Ov
was and what to tell him, just in case. They parted with lov-
ing embraces.

Finally she told Iziezi about the long hike she planned to
take in the mountains.

"Akidan is going with you," Iziezi said with a cheerful
smile.

Akidan was out with friends. The two women were eating dinner together at the table in the red-carpeted corner of
Iziezi's immaculate kitchen. It was a 'little-feast' night: several small dishes, delicately intense in flavor, surrounding a
bland, creamy pile of tuzi. It reminded Sutty of the food of

her far-off childhood. "You'd like basmati rice, Iziezi!" she said. Then she heard what her friend had said.

"Into the mountains? But it— We may be gone a long time."

"He's been up in the hills several times. He'll be seventeen this summer."

"But what will you do?" Akidan ran his aunt's errands, did her shopping, sweeping, fetching and carrying, helped her when a crutch slipped.

"My cousin's daughter will come stay with me."

"Mizi? But she's only six!"

"She's a help."

"Iziezi, I don't know if this is a good idea. I may go a long way. Even stay the winter in one of the villages up there."

"Dear Sutty, Ki isn't your responsibility. Maz Odiedin Manma told him to come. To go with a teacher to the Lap of Silong is the dream of his life. He wants to be a maz. Of course he has to grow up and find a partner. Maybe finding a partner is what he's mostly thinking about, just now." She smiled a little, not so cheerfully. "His parents were maz," she said.

"Your sister?"

"She was Maz Ariezi Meneng." She used the forbidden pronoun, she/he/they. Her face had fallen into its set expression of pain. "They were young," she said. A long pause. "Ki's father, Meneng Ariezi, everybody loved him. He was like the old heroes, like Penan Teran, so handsome and brave. . . . He thought being a maz was like armor. He believed nothing could hurt her/him/them. There was a while, then, three or four years, when things were going along more like the old days. No arrests. No more troops of young people from down there breaking windows, painting everything white, shouting. . . . It quieted down. The police didn't come here much. We all thought it was over, it would go back to being like it used to be. Then all of a sudden there were a lot of them. That's how they are. All of a sudden. They said there were, you know, too many people here breaking the law, reading, telling. . . . They said they'd clean the city. They paid skuyen to inform on people. I knew people who took their money." Her face was tight, closed. "A lot of people got arrested. My sister and her husband. They took them to a place called Erriak. Somewhere way off, down there. An island, I think. An island in the sea. A rehabilitation center. Five years ago we heard that Ariezi was dead. A notice came. We never have heard anything about Meneng Ariezi. Maybe he's still alive."

"How long ago. . . ?"

"Twelve years."

"Ki was four?"

"Nearly five. He remembers them a little. I try to help him remember them. I tell him about them."

Sutty said nothing for a while. She cleared the table, came and sat down again. "Iziezi, you're my friend. He's your child. He *is* my responsibility. It could be dangerous. They could follow us."

"Nobody follows the people of the Mountain to the Mountain, dear Sutty."

They all had that serene, foolhardy confidence when they talked about the mountains. No blame. Nothing to fear. Maybe they had to think that way in order to go on at all.

Sutty bought a nearly weightless, miraculously insulated sleeping bag for herself, and one for Akidan. Iziezi protested pro forma. Akidan was delighted and, like a child, slept in his sleeping bag from that night on, sweltering.

She got her boots and fleeces out again, packed her back-pack, and in the early morning of the appointed day walked with Akidan to the gathering place. It was spring on the edge of summer. The streets were dim blue in morning twilight, but up there to the northwest the great wall stood daylit, the peak was flying its radiant banners. We're going there, Sutty thought, we're going *there!* And she looked down to see if she was walking on the earth or on the air.

———

Vast slopes rose up all round to hanging glaciers and the glare of hidden ice fields. Their group of eight trudged along in line, so tiny in such hugeness that they seemed to be walking in place. Far up above them wheeled two geyma, the long-winged carrion birds that dwelt only among the high peaks, and flew always in pairs.

Six had set out: Sutty, Odiedin, Akidan, a young woman named Kieri, and a maz couple in their thirties, Tobadan and Siez. In a hill village four days out from Okzat-Ozkat two guides had joined them, shy, gentle-mannered men with weathered faces, whose age was hard to determine—somewhere between thirty and seventy. They were named Ieyu and Long.

The group had gone up and down in those hills for a week before they ever came to what these people called mountains. Then they had begun to climb. They had climbed steadily, daily, for eleven days now.

The luminous wall of Silong looked exactly the same, no nearer. A couple of insignificant 5,000-meter peaks to the north had shifted place and shrunk a bit. The guides and the three maz, with their trained memory for descriptive details and figures, knew the names and heights of all the peaks. They used a measure of altitude, pieng. As well as Sutty could recall, 15,000 pieng was about 5,000 meters; but since she wasn't certain her memory was correct, she mostly left the figures in pieng. She liked hearing these great heights, but she did not try to remember them, or the names of the mountains and passes. She had resolved before they set out never to ask where they were, where they were going, or how far they had yet to go. She had held to that resolve the more easily as it left her childishly free.

There was no trail as such except near villages, but there were charts that like river pilots' charts gave the course by landmarks and alignments: *When the north scarp of Mien falls behind the Ears of Taziu* . . . Odiedin and the other maz pored over these charts nightly with the two guides who had joined them in the foothills. Sutty listened to the poetry of the words. She did not ask the names of the tiny villages they passed through. If the Corporation, or even the Ekumen, ever demanded to know the way to the Lap of Silong, she could say in all truth that she did not know it.

She didn't know even the name of the place they were going to. She had heard it called the Mountain, Silong, the Lap of Silong, the Taproot, the High Umyazu. Possibly there was more than one place. She knew nothing about it. She resisted her desire to learn the name for everything, the word for everything. She was living among people to whom the highest spiritual attainment was to speak the world truly, and who had been silenced. Here, in this greater silence, where they could speak, she wanted to learn to listen to them. Not to question, only to listen. They had shared with her the sweetness of ordinary life lived mindfully. Now she shared with them the hard climb to the heights.

She had worried about her fitness for this trek. A month in the hill country of Ladakh and a few hiking holidays in the Chilean Andes were the sum of her mountaineering, and those had not been climbs, just steep walking. That was what they were doing now, but she wondered how high they would go. She had never walked above 4,000 meters. So far, though they must be that high by now, she had had no trouble except for running short of breath on stiff uphill stretches. Even Odiedin and the guides took it slow when the way got steep. Only Akidan and Kieri, a tough, rotund girl of twenty or so, raced up the endless slopes, and danced on outcroppings of granite over vast blue abysses, and were never out of breath. The eberdibi, the others called them — the kids, the calves.

They had walked a long day to get to a summer village: six or seven stone rings with yurts set up on them among steep, stony pastures tucked in the shelter of a huge curtain wall of granite. Sutty had been amazed to find how many people lived up here where it seemed there was nothing to live on but air and ice and rock. The vast, barren-seeming foothills far above Okzat-Ozkat had turned out to be full of villages, pasturages, small stone-walled fields. Even here among the high peaks there were habitations, the summer villages. Villagers came up from the hills through the late spring snow with their animals, the kind of eberdin called minule. Horned, half wild, with long legs and long pale wool, the minule pastured as high as grass grew and bore their young in the highest alpine meadows. Their fine, silky fleece was valuable even now in the days of artificial fibers. The villagers sold their wool, drank their milk, tanned their hides for shoes and clothing, burned their dung for fuel.

These people had lived this way forever. To them Okzat-Ozkat, a far provincial outpost of civilisation, was civilisation.

They were all Rangma. They spoke some Dovzan in the
foothills, and Sutty could converse well enough with Ieyu
and Long; but up here, though her Rangma had improved
greatly over the winter, she had to struggle to understand the
mountain dialect.

The villagers all turned out to welcome the visitors, a
jumble of dirty sunburnt smiling faces, racing children, shy
babies laced into leather cocoons and hung up on stakes like
little trophies, blatting minule with their white, silent, newborn young. Life, life abounding in the high, empty places.

Overhead, as always, were a couple of geyma spiraling
lazily on slender dark wings in the dark dazzling blue.

Odiedin and the young maz couple, Siez and Tobadan,
were already busy blessing huts and babies and livestock,
salving sores and smoke-damaged eyes, and telling The
blessing, if that was the right word for it—the word they
used meant something like including or bringing in—consisted of ritual chanting to the tabatt-batt-batt of the little
drum, and handing out slips of red or blue paper on which
the maz wrote the recipient's name and age and whatever
autobiographical facts they asked to have written, such as—

"Married with Temazi this winter."

"Built my house in the village."

"Bore a son this winter past. He lived one day and night.
His name was Enu."

"Twenty-two minulibi born this season to my flock."

"I am Ibien. I was six years old this spring."

As far as she could tell, the villagers could read only a few characters or none at all. They handled the written slips of paper with awe and deep satisfaction. They examined them for a long time from every direction, folded them carefully, slipped them into special pouches or finely decorated boxes in their house or tent. The maz had done a blessing or ingathering like this in every village they passed through that did not have a maz of its own. Some of the telling boxes in village houses, magnificently carved and decorated, had hundreds of these little red and blue record slips in them, tellings of lives present, lives past.

Odiedin was writing these for a family, Tobadan was dispensing herbs and salve to another family, and Siez, having finished the chant, had sat down with the rest of the population to tell. A narrow-eyed, taciturn young man, Siez in the villages became a fountain of words.

Tired and a little buzzy-headed—they must have come up another kilometer today—and liking the warmth of the afternoon sun, Sutty joined the half circle of intently gazing men and women and children, cross-legged on the stony dust, and listened with them.

"The telling!" Siez said, loudly, impressively, and paused.

His audience made a soft sound, *ah, ah,* and murmured to one another.

"The telling of a story!"

Ah, ah, murmur, murmur.

"The story is of Dear Takieki!"

Yes, yes. The dear Takieki, yes.

"Now the story begins! Now, the story begins when dear Takieki was still living with his old mother, being a grown man, but foolish. His mother died. She was poor. All she had to leave him was a sack of bean meal that she had been saving for them to eat in the winter. The landlord came and drove Takieki out of the house."

Ah, ah, the listeners murmured, nodding sadly.

"So there went Takieki walking down the road with the sack of bean meal slung over his shoulder. He walked and he walked, and on the next hill, walking toward him, he saw a ragged man. They met in the road. The man said, 'That's a heavy sack you carry, young man. Will you show me what is in it?' So Takieki did that. 'Bean meal!' says the ragged man."

Bean meal, whispered a child.

"'And what fine bean meal it is! But it'll never last you through the winter. I'll make a bargain with you, young man. I'll give you a real brass button for that bean meal!'

"'Oh, ho,' says Takieki, 'you think you're going to cheat me, but I'm not so foolish as that!'"

Ah, ah.

"So Takieki hoisted his sack and went on. And he walked and he walked, and on the next hill, coming toward him, he saw a ragged girl. They met in the road, and the girl said, 'A heavy sack you're carrying, young man. How strong you must be! May I see what's in it?' So Takieki showed her the bean meal, and she said, 'Fine bean meal! If you'll share it with me, young man, I'll go along with you, and I'll make love with you whenever you like, as long as the bean meal lasts.'"

A woman nudged the woman sitting by her, grinning.

"'Oh, ho,' says Takieki, 'you think you're going to cheat me, but I'm not so foolish as that!'

"And he slung his sack over his shoulder and went on. And he walked and he walked, and on the next hill, coming toward him, he saw a man and woman."

Ah, ah, very softly.

"The man was dark as dusk and the woman bright as dawn, and they wore clothing all of bright colors and jewels of bright colors, red, blue. They met in the road, and he/she/ they said, 'What a heavy sack you carry, young man. Will you show us what's in it?' So Takieki did that. Then the maz said, 'What fine bean meal! But it will never last you through the winter.' Takieki did not know what to say. The maz said, 'Dear Takieki, if you give us the sack of bean meal your mother gave you, you may have the farm that lies over that hill, with five barns full of grain, and five storehouses full of meal, and five stables full of eberdin. Five great rooms are in the farmhouse, and its roof is of coins of gold. And the mistress of the house is in the house, waiting to be your wife.'

"'Oh, ho,' said Takieki. 'You think you're going to cheat me, but I'm not so foolish as that!'

"And he walked on and he walked on, over the hill, past the farm with five barns and five storehouses and five stables

and a roof of gold, and so he went walking on, the dear
Takieki."

Ah, ah, ah! said all the listeners, with deep contentment.
And they relaxed from their intensity of listening, and chat-
ted a little, and brought Siez a cup and a pot of hot tea so that
he could refresh himself, and waited respectfully for whatever he would tell next.

Why was Takieki 'dear'? Sutty wondered. Because he was
foolish? (Bare feet standing on air.) Because he was wise? But
would a wise man have distrusted the maz? Surely he was
foolish to turn down the farm and five barns and a wife. Did
the story mean that to a holy man a farm and barns and a wife
aren't worth a bag of bean meal? Or did it mean that a holy
man, an ascetic, is a fool? The people she had lived with this
year honored self-restraint but did not admire self-depriva-
tion. They had no strenuous notions of fasting, and saw no
virtue whatever in discomfort, hunger, poverty.

If it had been a Terran parable, most likely Takieki ought
to have given the ragged man the bean meal for the brass button, or just given it for nothing, and then when he died he'd
get his reward in heaven. But on Aka, reward, whether spiritual or fiscal, was immediate. By his performance of a maz's
duties, Siez was not building up a bank account of virtue or
sanctity; in return for his story-telling he would receive
praise, shelter, dinner, supplies for their journey, and the
knowledge that he had done his job. Exercises were per-

formed not to attain an ideal of health or longevity but to achieve immediate well-being and for the pleasure of doing them. Meditation aimed toward a present and impermanent transcendance, not an ultimate nirvana. Aka was a cash, not a credit, economy.

Therefore their hatred of usury. A fair bargain and payment on the spot.

But then, what about the girl who offered to share what she had if he'd share what he had. Wasn't that a fair bargain?

Sutty puzzled over it all through the next tale, a famous bit of *The Valley War* that she had heard Siez tell several times in villages in the foothills—"I can tell that one when I'm sound asleep," he said. She decided that a good deal depended on how aware Takieki was of his own simplicity. Did he know the girl might trick him? Did he know he wasn't capable of managing a big farm? Maybe he did the right thing, hanging on to what his mother gave him. Maybe not.

As soon as the sun dropped behind the mountain wall to the west, the air in that vast shadow dropped below freezing. Everyone huddled into the hut-tents to eat, choking in the smoke and reek. The travelers would sleep in their own tents set up alongside the villagers' larger ones. The villagers would sleep naked, unwashed, promiscuous under heaps of silken pelts full of grease and fleas. In the tent she shared with Odiedin, Sutty thought about them before she slept. Brutal people, primitive people, the Monitor had said, leaning on the rail of the riverboat, looking up the long dark rise of the land that hid the Mountain. He was right. They were primitive, dirty, illiterate, ignorant, superstitious. They refused progress, hid from it, knew nothing of the March to the Stars. They hung on to their sack of bean meal.

———

Ten days or so after that, camped on névé in a long, shallow valley among pale cliffs and glaciers, Sutty heard an engine, an airplane or helicopter. The sound was distorted by wind and echoes. It might have been quite near or bounced from mountainside to mountainside from a long way off. There was ground fog blowing in tatters, a high overcast. Their tents, dun-colored, in the lee of an icefall, might be invisible in the vast landscape or might be plain to see from the air. They all held still as long as they could hear the stutter and rattle in the wind.

That was a weird place, the long valley. Icy air flowed down into it from the glaciers and pooled on its floor. Ghosts of mist snaked over the dead white snow.

Their food supplies were low. Sutty thought they must be close to their goal.

Instead of climbing up out of the long valley as she had expected, they descended from it on a long, wide slope of boulders. The wind blew without a pause and so hard that the gravel chattered ceaselessly against the larger stones.

Every step was difficult, and every breath. Looking up now they saw Silong palpably nearer, the great barrier wall reaching across the sky. But the bannered crest still stood remote behind it. All Sutty's dreams that night were of a voice she could hear but could not understand, a jewel she had found but could not touch.

The next day they kept going down, down steeply, to the southwest. A chant formed itself in Sutty's dulled mind: *Go back to go forward, fail to succeed. Go down to go upward, fail to succeed.* It would not get out of her head but thumped itself over and over at every jolting step. Go *down* to go *up*ward, *fail* to suc*ceed.* . . .

They came to a path across the slope of stones, then to a road, to a wall of stones, to a building of stone. Was this their journey's end? Was this the Lap of the Mother? But it was only a stopping place, a shelter. Maybe it had been an umyazu once. It was silent now. It held no stories. They stayed two days and nights in the cheerless house, resting, sleeping in their sleeping bags. There was nothing to make a fire with, only their tiny cookers, and no food left but dried smoked fish, which they shared out in little portions, soaking it in boiled snow to make soup.

"They'll come," people said. She did not ask who. She was so tired, she thought she could lie forever in the stone house, like one of the inhabitants of the little white stone houses in the cities of the dead she had seen in South America, resting in peace. Her own people burned their dead. She had always dreaded fire. This was better, the cold silence.

On the third morning she heard bells, a long way off, a faint jangling of little bells. "Come see, Sutty," Kieri said, and coaxed her to get up and stand in the door of the stone house and look out.

People were coming up from the south, winding among the grey boulders that stood higher than they did, people leading minule laden with packs on high saddles. There were poles fixed to the saddles, and from them long red and blue ribbons snapped in the wind. Clusters of little bells were tied into the white neck wool of the young animals that ran beside their mothers.

The next day they started down with the people and the animals to their summer village. It took them three days, but the going was mostly easy. The villagers wanted Sutty to ride one of the minule, but nobody else was riding. She walked. At one place they had to round a cliff under a precipice that continued vertically down from the narrow ledge of the pathway. The path was level, but no wider than a foot's breadth in places, and the snow on it was softened and loosened by the summer thaw. There they let the minule loose and instead of leading them followed them. They showed Sutty that she should put her feet in the animals' tracks. She followed one minule meticulously, step by step. Its woolly buttocks swaying nonchalantly, it sauntered along, pausing now and then to look down the sheer drop into the hazy depths with a bored expression. Nobody said anything till they were all off the cliff path. Then there was some laughter and joking, and several villagers made the mountain-heart gesture to Silong.

Down in the village the horned peak could not be seen, only the big shoulder of a nearer mountain and a glimpse of the barrier wall closing off the northwestern sky. The village was in a green place, open to north and south, good summer pasturage, sheltered, idyllic. Trees grew by the river: Odiedin showed them to her. They were as tall as her little finger. Down in Okzat-Ozkat such trees were the shrubs beside the Ereha. In the parks of Dovza City she had walked in their deep shade.

There had been a death among the people, a young man who had neglected a cut on his foot and died of blood poisoning. They had kept the body frozen in snow till the maz could come and perform his funeral. How had they known Odiedin's group was coming? How had these arrangements been made? She didn't understand, but she didn't think about it much. Here in the mountains there was much she didn't understand. She went along in the moment, like a child. "Tumble and spin and be helpless, like a baby...." Who had said that to her? She was content to walk, content to sit in the sun, content to follow in the footsteps of an animal. *Where my guides lead me in kindness, I follow, follow lightly* . . .

The two young maz told the funeral. That was how the

people spoke of it. Like all the rites, it was a narrative. For two days Siez and Tobadan sat with the man's father and aunt, his sister, his friends, a woman who had been married to him for a while, hearing everybody who wanted to talk about him tell them who he had been, what he had done. Now the two young men retold all that, ceremonially and in the formal language, to the soft batt-tabatt of the drum, passing the word one to the other across the body wrapped in white, thin, still-frozen cloth: a praise-song, gathering a life up into words, making it part of the endless telling.

Then Siez recited in his beautiful voice the ending of the story of Penan Teran, a mythic hero couple dear to the Rangma people. Penan and Teran were men of Silong, young warriors who rode the north wind, saddling the wind from the mountains like an eberdin and riding it down to battle, banners flying, to fight the ancient enemy of the Rangma, the sea people, the barbarians of the western plains. But Teran was killed in battle. And Penan led his people out of danger and then saddled the south wind, the sea wind, and rode it up into the mountains, where he leapt from the wind and died.

The people listened and wept, and there were tears in Sutty's eyes.

Then Tobadan struck the drum as Sutty had never heard it struck, no soft heartbeat but a driving urgent rhythm, to which people lifted up the body and carried it away in procession, swiftly away from the village, always with the drum beating.

"Where will they bury him?" she asked Odiedin.

"In the bellies of the geyma," Odiedin said. He pointed to distant rock spires on one of the mighty slopes above the valley. "They'll leave him naked there."

That was better than lying in a stone house, Sutty thought. Better far than fire.

"So he'll ride the wind," she said.

Odiedin looked up at her and after a while quietly assented.

Odiedin never said much, and what he said was often dry; he was not a mild man; but she was by now altogether at ease with him and he with her. He was writing on the little slips of blue and red paper, of which he had a seemingly endless supply in his pack: writing the name and family names of the man who had died, she saw, for those who mourned him to take home and keep in their telling boxes.

"Maz," she said. "Before the Dovzans became so powerful . . . before they began changing everything, using machinery, making things in factories instead of by hand, making new laws—all that—" Odiedin nodded. "It was after people from the Ekumen came here that they began that. Only about a lifetime ago. What were the Dovzans before that?"

"Barbarians."

He was a Rangma; he hadn't been able to resist saying it, saying it loud and clear. But she knew he was also a thoughtful, truthful man.

"Were they ignorant of the Telling?"

A pause. He set his pen down. "Long ago, yes. In the time of Penan Teran, yes. When *The Arbor* was written, yes. Then the people from the central plains, from Doy, began taming them. Trading with them, teaching them. So they learned to read and write and tell. But they were still barbarians, yoz Sutty. They'd rather make war than trade. When they traded, they made a war of it. They allowed usury, and sought great profits. They always had headmen to whom they paid tribute, men who were rich, and passed power down to their sons. Gobcy—bosses. So when they began to have maz, they made the maz into bosses, with the power to rule and punish. Gave the maz the power to tax. They made them rich. They made the sons of maz all maz, by birth. They made the ordinary people into nothing. It was wrong. It was all wrong."

"Maz Uming Ottiar spoke of that time once. As if he remembered it."

Odiedin nodded. "I remember the end of it. It was a bad time. Not as bad as this," he added, with his brief, harsh laugh.

"But this time came from that time. Grew out of it. Didn't it?"

He looked dubious, thoughtful.

"Why don't you tell of it?"

No response.

"You don't tell it, maz. It's never part of all the histories and tales you tell about the whole world all through the ages.

You tell about the far past. And you tell things from your own years, from ordinary people's lives—at funerals, and when children speak their tellings. But you don't tell about these great events. Nothing about how the world has changed in the last hundred years."

"None of that is part of the Telling," Odiedin said after a tense, pondering silence. "We tell what is right, what goes right, as it should go. Not what goes wrong."

"Penan Teran lost their battle, a battle with Dovza. It didn't go right, maz. But you tell it."

He looked up and studied her, not aggressively or with resentment, but from a very great distance. She had no idea what he was thinking or feeling, what he would say.

In the end he said only, "Ah."

The land mine going off? or the soft assent of the listener? She did not know.

He bent his head and wrote the name of the dead man, three bold, elegant characters across the slip of faded red paper. He had ground his ink from a block he carried, mixed it with river water in a tiny stoneware pot. The pen he was using for this writing was a geyma feather, ash-grey. He might have sat here cross-legged on the stony dust, writing a name, three hundred years ago. Three thousand years ago.

She had no business asking him what she had asked him. Wrong, wrong.

But the next day he said to her, "Maybe you've heard the Riddles of the Telling, yoz Sutty?"

"I don't think so."

"Children learn them. They're very old. What children tell is always the same. *What's the end of a story? When you begin telling it.* That's one of them."

"More a paradox than a riddle," Sutty said, thinking it over. "So the events must be over before the telling begins?"

Odiedin looked mildly surprised, as the maz generally did when she tried to interpret a saying or tale.

"That's not what it means," she said with resignation.

"It might mean that," he said. And after a while, "Penan leapt from the wind and died: that is Teran's story."

She had thought he was answering her question about why the maz did not tell about the Corporation State and the abuses that had preceded it. What did the ancient heroes have to do with that?

There was a gap between her mind and Odiedin's so wide light would need years to cross it.

"So the story went right, it's right to tell it; you see?" Odiedin said.

"I'm trying to see," she said.

———

They stayed six days in the summer village in the deep valley, resting. Then they set off again with new provisions and two new guides, north and up. And up, and up. Sutty kept no count of the days. Dawn came, they got up, the sun shone on them and on the endless slopes of rock and snow, and they walked. Dusk came, they camped, the sound of water ceased as the little thaw streams froze again, and they slept.

The air was thin, the way was steep. To the left, towering over them, rose the scarps and slopes of the mountain they were on. Behind them and to the right, peak after far peak rose out of mist and shadow into light, a motionless sea of icy broken waves to the remote horizon. The sun beat like a white drum in the dark blue sky. It was midsummer, avalanche season. They went very soft and silent among the unbalanced giants. Again and again in the daytime the silence quivered into a long, shuddering boom, multiplied and made sourceless by echoes.

Sutty heard people say the name of the mountain they were on, Zubuam. A Rangma word: Thunderer.

They had not seen Silong since they left the deep village. Zubuam's vast, deeply scored bulk closed off all the west. They inched along, north and up, north and up, in and out of the enormous wrinkles of the mountain's flank.

Breathing was slow work.

One night it began to snow. It snowed lightly but steadily all the next day.

Odiedin and the two guides who had joined them at the deep village squatted outside the tents that evening and conferred, sketching out lines, paths, zigzags on the snow with gloved fingers. Next morning the sun leapt brilliant over the

icy sea of the eastern peaks. They inched on, sweating, north
and up.

One morning as they walked, Sutty realised they were
turning their backs to the sun. Two days they went northwest, crawling around the immense shoulder of Zubuam.
On the third day at noon they turned a corner of rock and
ice. Before them the immense barrier faced them across a
vast abyss of air: Silong breaking like a white wave from the
depths to the regions of light. The day was diamond-bright
and still. The tip of the horned peak could be seen above the
ramparts. From it the faintest gossamer wisp of silver trailed
to the north.

The south wind was blowing, the wind Penan had leapt
from to die.

"Not far now," Siez said as they trudged on, southwest-
ward and down.

"I think I could walk here forever," Sutty said, and her
mind said, *I will. . . .*

During their stay in the deep village, Kieri had moved
into her tent. They had been the only women in the group
before the new guides joined them. Until then Sutty had
shared Odiedin's tent. A widowed maz, celibate, silent,
orderly, he had been a self-effacing, reassuring presence.
Sutty was reluctant to make the change, but Kieri pressed
her to. Kieri had tented with Akidan till then and was sick of
it. She told Sutty, "Ki's seventeen, he's in rut all the time. I

don't like boys! I like men and women! I want to sleep with you. Do you want to? Maz Odiedin can share with Ki."

Her use of the words was specific: *share* meant share the tent, *sleep* meant join the sleeping bags.

When she realised that, Sutty was more hesitant than ever; but the passivity she had encouraged in herself during the whole of this journey was stronger than her hesitations, and she agreed. Nothing about sex had mattered much to her since Pao's death. Sometimes her body craved to be touched and roused. Sex was something people wanted and needed. She could respond physically, so long as that was all they asked.

Kieri was strong, soft, warm, and as clean as any of them could be in the circumstances. "Let's heat up!" she said every night as she got into their joined sleeping bags. She made love to Sutty briefly and energetically and then fell asleep pressed up close against her. They were like two logs in a glowing campfire, burning down, Sutty thought, sinking asleep in the deep warmth.

Akidan had been honored to share the tent with his master and teacher, but he was miffed or frustrated by Kieri's desertion. He moped around her for a day or two, and then became attentive to the woman who had joined them in the village. The new guides were a brother and sister, a long-legged, round-faced, tireless pair in their twenties, named Naba and Shui. After a day or so Ki moved in with Shui. Odiedin, patient, invited Naba to share his tent.

What had Diodi the barrow man said, years ago, light-

years away, back down there in the streets where people
lived? "Sex for three hundred years! After three-hundred-year
sex anybody can fly!"

I can fly, Sutty thought, plodding on, southward and
down. There's nothing really in the world but stone and light.
All the other things, all the things, dissolve back into the two,
the stone, the light, and the two back into the one, the flying. . . . And then it will all be born again, it is born again,
always, in every moment it's being born, but all the time there's
only the one, the flying. . . . She plodded on through glory.

They came to the Lap of the Earth.

Though she knew it was implausible, impossible, foolish,
Sutty's imagination had insisted all along that the goal of
their journey was a great temple, a mysterious city hidden at
the top of the world, stone ramparts, flags flying, priests
chanting, gold and gongs and processions. All the imagery of
lost Lhasa, Dragon-Tiger Mountain, Machu Picchu. All the
ruins of the Earth.

They came steeply down the western flanks of Zubuam
for three days in cloudy weather, seldom able to see the barrier wall of Silong across the vast gulf of air where the wind
chased coiling clouds and ghostly snow flurries that never
came to earth. They followed the guides all one day through
cloud and fog along an arête, a long spine of snow-covered
rock with a steep drop to either side.

The weather cleared suddenly, clouds gone, sun blazing
at the zenith. Sutty was disoriented, looking up for the barrier

wall and not finding it. Odiedin came beside her. He said, smiling, "We're on Silong."

They had crossed over. The enormous mass of rock and ice behind them in the east was Zubuam. An avalanche went curling and smoking down a slanting face of the rock far up on the mountain. A long time later they heard the deep roar of it, the Thunderer telling them what it had to tell.

Zubuam and Silong, they were two and one, too. Old maz mountains. Old lovers.

She looked up at Silong. The heights of the barrier wall loomed directly over them, hiding the summit peak. Sky was a brilliant, jagged-edged slash from north to south.

Odiedin was pointing to the south. She looked and saw only rock, ice, the glitter of thaw water. No towers, no banners.

They set off, trudging along. They were on a path, level and quite clear, marked here and there with piles of flat stones. Often Sutty saw the dry, neat pellets of minule dung beside the way.

In mid-afternoon she made out a pair of rock spires that stuck up from a projecting corner of the mountain ahead like tusks from the lower jaw of a skull. The path narrowed as they got closer to this corner, becoming a ledge along a sheer cliff. When they got to the corner, the two reddish tusks of rock stood before them like a gateway, the path leading between them.

Here they stopped. Tobadan brought out his drum and patted it, and the three maz spoke and chanted. The words were all in Rangma and so old or so formalised that Sutty could not follow their meaning. The two guides from the village and their own guides delved into their packs and brought out little bundles of twigs tied with red and blue thread. They gave them to the maz, who received them with the mountain-heart gesture, facing toward Silong. They set them afire and fixed them among rocks by the pathway to burn down. The smoke smelled like sage, a dry incense. It curled small and blue and lazy among the rocks and along the path. The wind whistled by, a river of turbulent air rushing through the great gap between the mountains, but here in this gateway Silong sheltered them and there was no wind at all.

They picked up their packs and fell into line again, passing between the saber-tooth rocks. The path now bent back inward toward the slope of the mountain, and Sutty saw that it led across a cirque, a level-floored half-moon bay in the mountainside. In the nearly vertical, curving inner wall, still a half kilo or so distant, were black spots or holes. There was some snow on the floor of the cirque, trodden in an arabesque of paths leading to and from these black holes in the mountain.

Caves, scarred Adien, the ex-miner, who had died of the jaundice in the winter, whispered in her mind. *Caves full of being*.

The air seemed to thicken like syrup and to quiver, to shake. She was dizzy. Wind roared in her ears, deep and shrill, terrible. But they were out of the wind, here in the sunlit air of the cirque. She turned back in confusion, then in terror looked upward for the rockslide clattering down upon her. Black shadows crossed the air, the roar and rattle were deafening. She cowered, covering her head with her arms.

Silence.

She looked up, stood up. The others were all standing, like her, statues in the bright sunlight, pools of black shadow at their feet.

Behind them, between the tusks, the gateway rocks, something hung or lay crumpled. It gleamed blindingly and was shadow-black, like a lander seen from the ship in space. A lander—a flyer—a helicopter. She saw the rotor vane jammed up against the outer rock spire. "O Ram," she said.

"Mother Silong," Shui whispered, her clenched hand at her heart.

Then they started back toward the gate, toward the thing, Akidan in the lead, running.

"Wait, Akidan!" Odiedin shouted, but the boy was already there at the thing, the wreck. He shouted something back. Odiedin broke into a run.

Sutty could not breathe. She had to stand a while and still her heart. The older of their guides from the foothill country, Long, a kind, shy man, stood beside her, also trembling, also trying to breathe evenly, easily. They had come down, but they were still at 18,000 pieng, she had heard Siez say, 6,000 meters, a thin air, a terribly thin air. She said the numbers in her head.

"You all right, yoz Long?"

"Yes. You all right, yoz Sutty?"

They went forward together.

She heard Kieri talking: "I saw it, I looked around—I couldn't believe it—it was trying to fly between the pillars—"

"No, I saw it, it was out there, coming up alongside the pass, coming after us, and then it seemed like a flaw of wind hit it, and tipped it sideways, and just threw it down between the rocks!" That was Akidan.

"She took it in her hands," said Naba, the man from the deep village.

The three maz were at the wreck, in it.

Shui was kneeling near it, smashing something furiously, methodically, with a rock. The remains of a transmitter, Sutty saw. Stone Age revenge, her mind said coldly.

Her mind seemed to be very cold, detached from the rest of her, as if frostbitten.

She went closer and looked at the smashed helicopter. It had burst open in a strange way. The pilot was hanging in his seat straps, almost upside down. His face was mostly hidden by a blood-soaked woollen scarf. She saw his eyes, bits of jelly.

On the stony ground, between Odiedin and Siez, another man lay. His eyes were alive. He was staring up at her. After a while she recognised him.

Tobadan, the healer, was quickly, lightly running his hands over the man's body and limbs, though surely he couldn't tell much through the heavy clothing. He kept talking as if to keep the man awake. "Can you take off your helmet?" he asked. After a while the man tried to comply, fumbling with the fastening. Tobadan helped him. He continued gazing up at Sutty with a look of dull puzzlement. His face, always set and hard, was now slack.

"Is he hurt?"

"Yes," Tobadan said. "This knee. His back. Not broken, I think."

"You were lucky," Sutty's cold mind said, speaking aloud.

The man stared, looked away, made a weak gesture, tried to sit up. Odiedin pressed down gently on his shoulders, saying, "Be quiet. Wait. Sutty, don't let him get up. We need to get the other man out. People will be here soon."

Looking back into the cirque, toward the caves, she saw little figures hurrying to them across the snow.

She took Odiedin's place, standing over the Monitor. He lay flat on the dirt with his arms crossed on his chest. He shuddered violently every now and then. She herself was shivering. Her teeth chattered. She wrapped her arms around her body.

"Your pilot is dead," she said.

He said nothing. He trembled.

Suddenly there were people around them. They worked with efficiency, strapping the man onto a makeshift stretcher and lifting it and setting off for the caves, all within a minute or two. Others carried the dead man. Some gathered around Odiedin and the young maz. There was a soft buzz of voices that did nothing but buzz in Sutty's head, meaningless as the speech of flies.

She looked for Long, joined him, and walked with him across the cirque. It was farther than it had seemed to the mountain wall and the entrance to the caves. Overhead a pair of geyma soared in long, lazy spirals. The sun was already behind the top of the barrier wall. Silong's vast shadow rose blue against Zubuam.

The caves were like nothing she had ever seen. There were many of them, hundreds, some tiny, no more than bubbles in the rock, some big as the doors of hangars. They made a lacework of circles interlocking and overlapping in the wall of rock, patterns, traceries. The edges of the entrances were fretted with clusters of lesser circles, silvery stone shining against black shadow, like soapsuds, like foam, like the edges of Mandelbrot figures.

Against one entrance a little fence had been set up. Sutty looked in as they passed, and the white face of a young minule looked back at her with dark, quiet eyes. There was a whole stable of the animals built back into the caves. She could smell the pungent, warm, grassy odor of them. The entrances to the caves had been widened and brought down to ground level where necessary, but they kept their circularity. The people she and Long were following entered one of these great round doors into the mountain. Inside, she looked back for a moment at the entrance and saw daylight as a blazing, perfect circle set in dead black.

SEVEN

IT WAS NOT a city with banners and golden processions, a temple with drums and bells and the chanting of priests. It was very cold, very dark, very poor. It was silent.

Food, bedding, oil for lamps, stoves and heating devices, everything that made it possible for anyone to live at the Lap of Silong had to be brought up from the eastern hill country on the backs of minules or human beings, little by little, in tiny caravans that would attract no attention, during the few months when it was possible to reach the place at all. In the summer thirty or forty men and women stayed there, living in the caves. Some of them brought books, papers, texts of the Telling. They stayed to arrange and protect all the books already there, the thousands and thousands of volumes brought over the decades from all over the great continent. They stayed to read and study, to be with the books, to be in the caves full of being.

Sutty moved in her first days there through a dream of darkness, strangeness. The caves themselves were bewildering: endless bubble chambers interconnecting, interfacing, dark walls, floors, ceilings all curved into one another seamlessly, so disorienting that sometimes she felt she was floating weightless. Sounds echoed so they had no direction. There was never enough light.

Her group of pilgrims set up their tents in a great vaulted chamber and slept in them, huddled into them for warmth as they had done during their trek. In other caves were other little constellations of tents. One maz couple had taken a three-meter, almost perfectly spherical hollow and made a private nest of it. Cookstoves and tables were in a large, flat-floored cave that received daylight through a couple of high vents, and everybody met there at mealtimes. The cooks scrupulously shared out the food. Never quite enough, and the same few things over and over: thin tea, boiled bean meal, dry cheese, dried leaves of spinach-like yota, a taste of hot pickle. Winter food, though it was summer. Food for the roots, for endurance.

The maz and the students and guides staying there this summer were all from the north and east, the vast hill countries and plains of the continent's center, Amareza, Doy,

Kangnegne. These maz were city people, far more learned and sophisticated than those of the little hill city Sutty knew. Trained in a profound and still unbroken intellectual and bodily and spiritual discipline, heirs to a tradition vaster, even in its ruin and enforced secrecy, than she had ever conceived, they had an impersonality about them as well as great personal authority. They did not play the pundit (Uncle Hurree's phrase), but even the mildest of them was surrounded by a kind of aura or field—Sutty hated such words yet had to use them—that kept one from informal approach. They were aloof, absorbed in the telling, the books, the treasures of the caves.

The morning after the newcomers' arrival, the maz named Igneba and Ikak took them to and through what they called the Library. Numbers daubed in luminous paint over the openings corresponded to a chart of the caves that the maz showed them. By going always to a lower number, if you lost your way in the labyrinth—and it was quite easy to do so—you would always return to the outer caves. The man, Igneba Ikak, carried an electric torch, but like so much Akan manufacture it was unreliable or defective and kept failing. Ikak Igneba carried an oil lantern. From it once or twice she lighted lamps hanging on the walls, to illuminate the caves of being, the round rooms full of words, where the Telling lay hidden, in silence. Under rock, under snow.

Books, thousands of books, in leather and cloth and wooden and paper bindings, unbound manuscripts in carved and painted boxes and jewelled caskets, fragments of ancient writing blazing with gold leaf, scrolls in tubes and boxes or tied with tape, books on vellum, parchment, rag paper, pulp paper, handwritten, printed, books on the floors, in boxes, in small crates, on rickety low shelves made of scrap wood from the crates. In one big cave the volumes stood ranked on two shelves, at waist height and eye level, dug into the walls right around the circumference. Those shelves were the work of long ago, Ikak said, carved by maz living here when it was a small umyazu and that one room had been all its library. Those maz had had the time and means for such work. Now all they could do was lay plastic sheeting to keep the books from the dirt or bare rock, stack or arrange them as best they could, try to sort them to some degree, and keep them hidden, keep them safe. Protect them, guard them, and, when there was time, read them.

But nobody in one lifetime could read more than a fragment of what was here, this broken labyrinth of words, this shattered, interrupted, immense story of a people and a world through the centuries, the millennia.

Odiedin sat down on the floor in one of the silent, gleamlit caves where the books stretched away from the entrance in rows, like rows of mown grass but dark, vanishing into darkness. He sat down between two rows on the stone floor, picked up a small book with a worn cloth cover, and held it in his lap. He bowed his head over it without opening it. Tears ran down his cheeks.

They were free to go into the book caves as they wanted. In the days that followed, Sutty went back and back, wandering with the small, keen beam of an oil lamp to guide her, settling down here and there to read. She had her noter with her and scanned into it what she read, often whole books she didn't have time to read. She read the texts of blessings, the protocols of ceremonies, recipes, prescriptions for curing cold sores and for living to a great age, stories, legends, annals, lives of famous maz, lives of obscure merchants, testimonies of people who lived thousands of years ago and a few years ago, tales of travel, meditations of mystics, treatises of philosophy and of mathematics, herbals, bestiaries, anatomies, geometries both real and metaphysical, maps of Aka, maps of imaginary worlds, histories of ancient lands, poems. All the poems in the world were here.

She knelt at a wooden crate filled with papers and worn, handmade books, the salvage of some small umyazu or town, saved from the bulldozer and the bonfire, carried here up the long hard ways of the Mountain to be safe, to be kept, to tell. By the light of her lamp on the rock floor she opened one of the books, a child's primer. The ideograms were written large and without any qualifiers of aspect, mood, number, and Element. On one page was a crude woodcut of a man fishing from a humpbacked bridge. THE MOUNTAIN IS THE MOTHER OF THE RIVER, said the ideograms beneath the picture.

She would stay in the caves reading till the words of the dead, the utter silence, the cold, the globe of darkness surrounding her, grew too strange, and she made her way back to daylight and the sound of living voices.

She knew now that all she would ever know of the Telling was the least hint or fragment of what there was to know. But that was all right; that was how it was. So long as it was here.

One maz couple was making a catalogue of the books in their Akan version of Sutty's noter. They had been coming up to the caves for twenty years, working on the catalogue. They discussed it with her eagerly, and she promised to try to link her noter with theirs to duplicate and transfer the information.

Though the maz treated her with unfailing courtesy and respect, conversations were mostly formal and often difficult. They all had to speak in a language not their own, Dovzan. Though the Akans spoke it in public in their lives 'down below,' it was not the language in which they thought, and not the language of the Telling. It was the tongue of the enemy. It was a barrier. Sutty realized how much closer she had drawn to people in Okzat-Ozkat as she learned their Rangma speech. Several of the maz of the Library knew Hainish, which was taught in the Corporation universities as a mark of true education. It wasn't of much use here, except perhaps in one conversation Sutty had with the young maz Unroy Kigno.

They went out together to enjoy the daylight for an hour and to sweep footsteps away. Since the helicopter had come so close, the first aircraft that had ever done so, the people of the Library took more care to sweep away paths or tracks in the snow that might lead an eye in the sky to the entrances of the caves. Sutty and Unroy had finished the rather pleasant job of throwing the light, dry snow about with brooms, and were taking a breather, sitting on boulders near the minules' stable.

"What is history?" Unroy asked abruptly, using the Hainish word. "Who are historians? Are you one?"

"The Hainish say I am," Sutty said, and they launched into a long and intense linguistico-philosophical discussion about whether history and the Telling could be understood as the same thing, or similar things, or not alike at all; about what historians did, what maz did, and why.

"I think history and the Telling are the same thing," Unroy said at last. "They're ways of holding and keeping things sacred."

"What is sacredness?"

"What is true is sacred. What has been suffered. What is beautiful."

"So the Telling tries to find the truth in events . . . or the pain, or the beauty?"

"No need to try to find it," said Unroy. "The sacredness is there. In the truth, the pain, the beauty. So that the telling of it is sacred."

Her partner, Kigno, was in a prison camp in Doy. He had been arrested and sentenced for teaching atheist religion and reactionary antiscience dogma. Unroy knew where he was, a huge steel-mill complex manned by prisoners, but no communication was possible.

"There are hundreds of thousands of people in the rehabilitation centers," Unroy told Sutty. "The Corporation gets its labor cheap."

"What are you going to do with your prisoner here?"

Unroy shook her head. "I wish he'd been killed like the other one," she said. "He's a problem we have no solution to."

Sutty agreed in bitter silence.

The Monitor was being well looked after; several of the maz were professional healers. They had put him in a small tent by himself and kept him warm and fed. His tent was in a big cave among seven or eight tents belonging to guides and minule hostlers. There was always somebody there with an ear and an eye, as they put it. In any case there was no danger of his trying to escape until his wrenched back and badly damaged knee mended.

Odiedin visited him daily. Sutty had not yet brought herself to do so.

"His name is Yara," Odiedin told her.

"His name is Monitor," she said, contemptuous.

"Not any longer," Odiedin said drily. "His pursuit of us was unauthorised. If he goes back to Dovza, he'll be sent to a rehabilitation center."

"A forced labor camp? Why?"

"Officials must not exceed their orders or take unauthorised action."

"That wasn't a Corporation helicopter?"

Odiedin shook his head. "The pilot owned it. Used it to

bring supplies to mountain climbers in the South Range. Yara hired him. To look for us."

"How strange," Sutty said. "Was he after me, then?"

"As a guide."

"I was afraid of that."

"I was not." Odiedin sighed. "The Corporation is so big, its apparatus is so clumsy, we little people in these big hills are beneath their notice. We slip through the mesh. Or we've done so for many years. So I didn't worry. But he wasn't the Corporation police. He was one man. One fanatic."

"Fanatic?" She laughed. "He believes slogans? He loves the Corporation?"

"He hates us. The maz, the Telling. He fears you."

"As an alien?"

"He thinks you'll persuade the Ekumen to side with the maz against the Corporation."

"What makes him think that?"

"I don't know. He's a strange man. I think you should talk with him."

"What for?"

"To hear what he has to tell," Odiedin said.

———

She put it off, but conscience pushed her. Odiedin was no scholar, no sage like these maz from the lowlands, but he had a clear mind and a clear heart. On their long trek she had come to trust him entirely, and when she saw him crying over the books in the Library, she knew she loved him. She wanted to do what he asked her to do, even if it was to hear what the Monitor had to tell.

Maybe she could also tell the Monitor a little of what he ought to hear. In any case, sooner or later she'd have to face him. And the question of what to do about him. And the question of her responsibility for his being there.

Before the evening meal the next day, she went to the big cave where they had put him. A couple of minule handlers were gambling, tossing marked sticks, by lantern light. On the inner wall of the cave, a pure black concave curve ten meters high, the figure of the Tree had been incised by the dwellers here in centuries past: the single trunk, the two branches, the five lobes of foliage. Gold leaf still glittered in the lines of the drawing, and bits of crystal, jet, and moonstone winked among the carved leaves. Her eyes were well used to darkness now. The glow of a small electric light in a tent close under the back wall seemed as bright as sunlight.

"The Dovzan?" she asked the gamblers. One nodded with his chin toward the lighted tent.

The door flap was closed. She stood outside a while and finally said, "Monitor?"

The flap opened. She looked in cautiously. The small interior of the tent was warm and bright. They had fixed the injured man a bed pad with a slanted back support so he need not lie entirely flat. The cord of the door flap, a hand-crank-powered electric lamp, a tiny oil heater, a bottle of water, and a small noter lay within his reach.

He had been terribly bruised in the crash, and the bruising was still livid: blue-black-green all down the right side of his face, the right eye swollen half shut, both arms spotted with great brown-blue marks. Two fingers of his left hand were lightly splinted. But Sutty's eyes were on the little device, the noter.

She entered the tent on her knees, and kneeling in the narrow clear space, picked up the device and studied it.

"It doesn't transmit," the man said.

"So you say," Sutty said, beginning to play with it, to run it through its paces. After a while she said, ironically, "Apologies for going through your private files, Monitor. I'm not interested in them. But I have to test this thing's capacities."

He said nothing.

The device was a recorder notebook, rather flashily designed but with several serious design flaws, like so much Akan technology—undigested techshit, she thought. It had no sending or receiving functions. She set it back down where he could reach it.

That alarm relieved, she was aware of her embarrassment and intense discomfort at being shut in this small space with this man. She wanted nothing but distance from him. The only way to make it was with words.

"What were you trying to do?"

"Follow you."

"Your government had ordered you not to."

After a pause he said, "I could not accept that."

"So the cog is wiser than the wheel?"

He said nothing. He had not moved at all since opening the door flap. The rigidity of his body probably signified pain. She observed it with no feeling.

"If you hadn't crashed, what would you have done? Flown back to Dovza and reported—what? Some cave mouths?"

He said nothing.

"What do you know about this place?"

As she asked the question, she realised that he had seen nothing of it but this one cave, a few hostlers, a few maz. He need never learn what it was. They could blindfold him—, probably no need even for that: just get him out, get him away as soon as he could be moved. He had seen nothing but a travelers' resting place. He had nothing to report.

"This is the Lap of Silong," he said. "The last Library."

"What makes you think that?" she said, made angry by disappointment.

"This is where you were coming. The Office of Ethical Purity has been looking for it for a long time. The place where they hide the books. This is it."

"Who are 'they,' Monitor?"

"The enemies of the state."

"O Ram!" she said. She sat back, as far from him as she could get, and hugged her knees. She spoke slowly, stopping after each sentence. "You people have learned everything we did wrong, and nothing we did right. I wish we'd never come to Aka. But since in our own stupid intellectual hubris we did so, we should either have refused you the information you demanded, or taught you Terran history. But of course you wouldn't have listened. You don't believe in history. You threw out your own history like garbage."

"It was garbage."

His brown skin was greyish where it wasn't black-and-blue. His voice was hoarse and dogged. The man is hurt and helpless, she thought with neither sympathy nor shame.

"I know who you are," she said. "You're my enemy. The true believer. The righteous man with the righteous mission. The one that jails people for reading and burns the books. That persecutes people who do exercises the wrong way. That dumps out the medicine and pisses on it. That pushes the button that sends the drones to drop the bombs. And hides behind a bunker and doesn't get hurt. Shielded by God. Or the state. Or whatever lie he uses to hide his envy and self-interest and cowardice and lust for power. It took me a while to see you, though. You saw me right away. You knew I was your enemy. Was unrighteous. How did you know it?"

"They sent you to the mountains," he said. He had been looking straight forward, but he turned his head stiffly now to meet her eyes. "To a place where you would meet the maz. I did not wish any harm to you, yoz."

After a moment she said, "Yoz!"

He had looked away again. She watched his swollen, unreadable face.

He reached out his good hand and began to pump the hand crank of his lamp up and down. The little square bulb inside it immediately brightened. For the hundredth time in a corner of her mind Sutty wondered why the Akans made their lightbulbs square. But the rest of her mind was full of shadows, anger, hate, contempt.

"Did your people let me go to Okzat-Ozkat as a decoy? A tool of your official ideologues? Were they hoping I'd lead them here?"

"I thought so," he said after a pause.

"But you told me to keep away from the maz!"

"I thought they were dangerous."

"To whom?"

"To . . . the Ekumen. And my government." He used the old word, and corrected it: "The Corporation."

"You don't make sense, Monitor."

He had stopped cranking the lamp. He looked straight ahead again.

"The pilot said, 'There they are,' and we came up alongside the path," he said. "And he shouted, and I saw your group on the path. And smoke, behind you, smoke coming out of the rocks. But we were being thrown sideways, into the mountain. Into the rocks. The helicopter was thrown. Pushed."

He held his injured left hand with his right hand, stiffly. He was controlling his shivering.

"Catabatic winds, yoz," Sutty said after a while, softly. "And very high altitude for a helicopter."

He nodded. He had told himself the same thing. Many times, no doubt.

"They hold this place sacred," she said.

Where did that word come from? Not a word she used. Why was she tormenting him? Wrong, wrong.

"Listen, Yara—that's your name?—don't let rotten-corpse superstition get hold of you. I don't think Mother Silong pays any attention to us at all."

He shook his head, mute. Maybe he had told himself that, too.

She did not know what else to say to him. After a long silence, he spoke.

"I deserve punishment," he said.

That shook her.

"Well, you got it," she said finally. "And you'll probably get more, one way or another. What are we going to do with you? That has to be decided. It's getting on into late summer. They're talking of leaving in a few weeks. So, until then you might as well take it easy. And get walking again. Because wherever you go from here, I don't think you'll be flying on the south wind."

He looked at her again. He was unmistakably frightened. By what she had said? By whatever guilt had made him say, "I deserve punishment"? Or merely because lying helpless among the enemy was a frightening job?

He gave his stiff, painful, single nod and said, "My knee will be healed soon."

As she went back through the caves, she thought that, grotesque as it seemed, there was something childlike about the man, something simple and pure. Then she said to herself, Simplistic, not simple, and what the hell does pure mean? Saintly, holy, all that stuff? (*Don't Mother-Teresa me, girl,* Uncle Hurree muttered in her mind.) He was simpleminded, with his 'enemy of the state' jargon. And singleminded. A fanatic, as Odiedin had said. In fact, a terrorist. Pure and simple.

Talking with him had soured her. She wished she had not done it, had not seen him. Anxiety and frustration made her impatient with her friends.

Kieri, with whom she still shared the tent, though not lately the sleeping bag, was cheerful and affectionate, but her self-confidence was impervious. Kieri knew all she wanted to know. All she wanted of the Telling was stories and superstitions. She had no interest in learning from the maz here and never went into the caves of books. She had come for the mere adventure.

Akidan, on the other hand, was in a state of hero worship fatally mixed with lust. The guide Shui had gone back to her village soon after they came to the caves, leaving Akidan in his tent alone, and he had immediately fallen in love with Maz Unroy Kigno. He stuck to her like a minule kid to its mother, gazed at her with worshiping eyes, memorised her every word. Unfortunately, the only people under the old system whose sexual life was strictly regulated were the maz. Lifelong monogamy was their rule, whether they were or were not with their partner. The maz Sutty had known, as far as she could see, lived by this rule. And Akidan, a gentle-natured young man, had no real intention of questioning or testing it. He was simply smitten, head over heels, a pitiful victim of hormone-driven hagiolatry.

Unroy was sorry for him but did not let him know it. She discouraged him harshly, challenging his self-discipline, his learning, his capacity to become a maz. When he made his infatuation too clear, she turned on him and quoted a well-known tag from *The Arbor*, "The two that are one are not two, but the one that is two is one. . . ." It seemed a fairly subtle reproof, but Akidan turned pale with shame and slunk away. He had been miserable ever since. Kieri talked with him a good deal and seemed inclined to comfort him. Sutty rather wished she would. She didn't want the seethe and sway of adolescent emotions; she wanted adult counsel, mature certainty. She felt that she must go forward and was at a dead end; must decide and did not know what was to be decided.

The Lap of Silong was wholly cut off from the rest of the world. No radios or any kind of communicators were ever brought there, lest signals be traced. News could come only up the northeastern paths or along the long, difficult way Sutty's party had come from the southeast. This late in the summer, it was most unlikely that anyone else would arrive;

indeed, as she had told the Monitor, the people here were already talking of leaving.

She listened to them discuss their plans. It was their custom to depart a few at a time and take different ways where the paths diverged. As soon as they could do so, they would join with the small caravans of summer-village people going down to the foothills. Thus the pilgrimage, the way to the caves, had been kept invisible for forty years.

It was already too late, Odiedin told her, to go back the way their group had come, on the southeast trail. The guides from the deep village had left for home promptly, and even so expected to meet storm and snow on Zubuam. The rest of them would have to go down into Amareza, the hill region northeast of Silong, and work their way around the end of the Headwaters Range and back up through the foothills to Okzat-Ozkat. On foot it would take a couple of months. Odiedin thought they could get lifts on trucks through the hill country, though they would have to split up into pairs to do so.

It all sounded frightening and improbable to Sutty. To follow her guides up into the mountains, to follow a hidden way through the clouds to a secret, sacred place, was one thing; to wander like a beggar, to hitchhike, anonymous and unprotected, in the vast countrysides of an alien world, was another thing altogether. She trusted Odiedin, yes, but she wanted very badly to get in touch with Tong Ov.

And what were they going to do with the Monitor? Let

him loose to run and blab to the bureaus and the ministries about the last great cache of banned books? He might be in terminal disgrace, but before his bosses sent him off to the salt mines, they'd hear what he had to report.

And what would she say to Tong Ov when and if she ever did talk to him again? He had sent her to find Aka's history, its lost, outlawed past, its true being, and she had found it. But then what?

What the maz wanted of her was clear and urgent: they wanted her to save their treasure. It was the only thing clear to her in the obscure turmoil of her thoughts and feelings since she had talked to the Monitor.

What she herself wanted—would have wanted, if it had been possible—was to stay here. To live in the caves of being, to read, to hear the Telling, here where it was still complete or nearly complete, still one unbroken story. To live in the forest of words. To listen. That was what she was fitted for, what she longed to do, and could not.

As the maz longed to do and could not.

"We were stupid, yoz Sutty," said Goiri Engnake, a maz from the great city of Kangnegne in the center of the continent, a scholar of philosophy who had served fourteen years in an agricultural labor camp for disseminating reactionary ideology. She was a worn, tough, abrupt woman. "Carrying everything up here. We should have left it all over the place. Left the books with whoever had the books, and made copies. Spent our time copying, instead of bringing everything we have together where they can destroy it all at once. But you see we're old-fashioned. People thought about how long it takes to copy, how dangerous it is to try to print. They didn't look at the machines the Corporation started making, the ways to copy things in an instant, to put whole libraries into a computer. Now we've got our treasure where we can't use those technologies. We can't bring a computer up here, and if we could, how would we power it? And how long would it take to put all this into it?"

"With Akan technology, years," Sutty said. "With what's available to the Ekumen, a summer, maybe."

Looking at Goiri's face, she added, slowly, "If we were authorised to do so. By the Corporation of Aka. And by the Stabiles of the Ekumen."

"I understand."

They were in the 'kitchen,' the cave where they cooked and ate. It was sealed to the extent that it could be kept habitably warm, and was the gathering place, at all hours, for discussions and conversations. They had eaten breakfast and were each nursing along a cup of very weak bezit tea. *It starts the flow and reunites*, Iziezi murmured in her mind.

"Would you ask the Envoy to request such authorisation, yoz?"

"Yes, of course," Sutty said. After a pause, "That is, I would ask him if he considered it feasible, or wise. If such a request indicated to your government that this place exists, we'd have blown your cover, maz."

Goiri grinned at Sutty's choice of words. They were of course speaking in Dovzan. "But maybe the fact that you know about it, that the Ekumen is interested in it, would protect the Library," she said. "Prevent them from sending the police here to destroy it."

"Maybe."

"The Executives of the Corporation hold the Ekumen in very high respect."

"Yes. They also hold its Envoys completely out of touch with everybody on Aka except ministers and bureaucrats. The Corporation has been given a great deal of useful information. In return, the Ekumen has been given a great deal of useless propaganda."

Goiri pondered this, and asked at last, "If you know that, why do you allow it?"

"Well, Maz Goiri, the Ekumen takes a very long view. So long that it's often hard for a short-lived being to live with. The principle we work on is that withholding knowledge is always a mistake—in the long run. So if asked to tell what we know, we tell it. To that extent, we're like you, maz."

"No longer," Goiri said bitterly. "All we know, we hide."

"You have no choice. Your bureaucrats are dangerous people. They're believers." Sutty sipped her tea. Her throat was dry. "On my world, when I was growing up, there was a powerful group of believers. They believed that their beliefs should prevail absolutely, that no other way of thinking should exist. They sabotaged the information storage networks and destroyed libraries and schools all over the world. They didn't destroy everything, of course. It can be pieced back together. But . . . damage was done. That kind of damage is something like a stroke. One recovers, almost. But you know all that."

She stopped. She was talking too much. Her voice was shaking. She was getting too close to it. Far too close to it. Wrong.

Goiri looked shaken too. "All I know of your world, yoz . . ."

"Is that we fly around in space ships bringing enlightenment to lesser, backward worlds," Sutty said. Then she slapped one hand on the table and the other across her mouth.

Goiri stared.

"It's a way the Rangma have of reminding themselves to shut up," Sutty said. She smiled, but her hands were shaking now.

They were both silent for a while.

"I thought of you . . . of all the people of the Ekumen, as very wise, above error. How childish," Goiri said. "How unfair."

Another silence.

"I'll do what I can, maz," Sutty said. "If and when I get back to Dovza City. It might not be safe to try to get in touch with the Mobile by telephone from Amareza. I could say, for the wiretappers, that we got lost trying to hike up to Silong and found an eastern path out of the mountains. But if I turn up in Amareza, where I wasn't authorised to go, they'll ask questions. I can clam up, but I don't think I can lie. I mean, not well. . . . And there's the problem of the Monitor."

"Yes. I wish you would talk to him, yoz Sutty."

Et tu, Brute? said Uncle Hurree, his eyebrows sarcastic.

"Why, Maz Goiri?"

"Well, he is—as you call it—a believer. And as you say, that's dangerous. Tell him what you told me about your Earth. Tell him more than you told me. Tell him that belief is the wound that knowledge heals."

Sutty drank the last of her tea. The taste was bitter, delicate. "I can't remember where I heard that. Not in a book. I heard it told."

"Teran said it to Penan. After he was wounded fighting the barbarians."

Sutty remembered now: the circle of mourners in the green valley under the great slopes of stone and snow, the body of the young man covered with thin, ice-white cloth, the voice of the maz telling the story.

Goiri said, "Teran was dying. He said, 'My brother, my husband, my love, my self, you and I believed that we would defeat our enemy and bring peace to our land. But belief is the wound that knowledge heals, and death begins the Telling of our life.' Then he died in Penan's arms."

The grave, yoz. Where it begins.

"I can carry that message," Sutty said finally. "Though bigots have small ears."

EIGHT

HIS TENT WAS lighted only by the faint glimmer of the heater. When she entered, he began pumping the little crank of the lantern. It took a long time to brighten, and the glow was small and feeble.

She sat down cross-legged in the empty half of the tent. As well as she could make out, his face was no longer swollen, though still discolored. The backboard was set so that he was sitting up almost straight.

"You lie here in the dark, night and day," she said. "It must be strange. Sensory deprivation. How do you pass the time?" She heard the cold sharpness of her voice.

"I sleep," he said. "I think."

"Therefore you are. . . . Do you recite slogans? Onward, upward, forward? Reactionary thought is the defeated enemy?"

He said nothing.

A book lay beside the bed pad. She picked it up. It was a schoolbook, a collection of poems, stories, exemplary lives, and so on, for children of ten or so. It took her some moments to realise that it was printed in ideograms, not in alphabet. She had practically forgotten that in the Monitor's world, in modern Aka, everything was in alphabet, that the ideograms were banned, illegal, unused, forgotten.

"Can you read this?" she demanded, startled and some-how unnerved.

"Odiedin Manma gave it to me."

"Can you read it?"

"Slowly."

"When did you learn to read rotten-corpse primitive anti-scientific writing, Monitor?"

"When I was a boy."

"Who taught you?"

"The people I lived with."

"Who were they?"

"My mother's parents."

His answers came always after a pause, and spoken low, almost mumbled, like the replies of a humiliated schoolboy to a goading questioner. Sutty was abruptly overcome with shame. She felt her cheeks burn, her head swim.

Wrong again. Worse than wrong.

After a prolonged silence she said, "I beg your pardon for the way I've been talking to you. I disliked your manner to me, on the boat and in Okzat-Ozkat. I came to hate you when I thought you responsible for destroying Maz Sotyu Ang's herbary, his lifework, his life. And for hounding my friends. And hounding me. I hate the bigotry you believe in. But I'll try not to hate you."

"Why?" he asked. His voice was cold, as she remembered it.

"Hate eats the hater," she quoted from a familiar text of the Telling.

He sat impassive, tense as always. She, however, began to relax. Her confession had relieved not only her shame but also the resentful oppression she had felt in his presence. She got her legs into a more comfortable semilotus, straightened her back. She was able to look at him instead of sneaking glances. She watched his rigid face for a while. He would not or could not say anything, but she could.

"They want me to talk to you," she said. "They want me to tell you what life is like on Terra. The sad and ugly truths you'll find at the end of the March to the Stars. So that maybe you'll begin to ask yourself that fatal question: Do I know what I'm doing? But you probably don't want to. . . . Also I'm curious about what life's like for someone like you. What makes a man a Monitor. Will you tell me? Why did you live with your grandparents? Why did you learn to read the

old writing? You're about forty, I should think. It was already
banned when you were a child, wasn't it?"

He nodded. She had put the book back down. He picked
it up, seeming to study the flowing calligraphy of the title on
the cover: JEWEL FRUITS FROM THE TREE OF LEARNING.

"Tell me," she said. "Where were you born?"

"Bolov Yeda. On the western coast."

"And they named you Yara—'Strong.'"

He shook his head. "They named me Azyaru," he said.

Azya Aru. She had been reading about them just a day or
so ago in a *History of the Western Lands*, which Unroy
showed her in one of their forays into the Library. A maz
couple of two centuries ago, Azya and Aru had been the
chief founders and apostles of the Telling in Dovza. The first
boss maz. Dovzan culture heroes, until the secularisation.
Under the Corporation, they had no doubt become culture
villains, until they could be totally erased, whited out,
deleted.

"Were your parents maz, then?"

"My grandparents." He held the book as if it were a talis-
man. "The first thing I remember is my grandfather showing
me how to write the word 'tree.'" His finger on the cover of
the book sketched the two-stroke ideogram. "We were sitting
on the porch, in the shade, where we could see the sea. The
fishing boats were coming in. Bolov Yeda is on hills above a
bay. The biggest city on the coast. My grandparents had a
beautiful house. There was a vine growing over the porch, up

to the roof, with a thick trunk and yellow flowers. They held the Telling in the house every day. They went to the umyazu in the evenings."

He used the forbidden pronoun, he/she/they. He was not aware of it, Sutty thought. His voice had become soft, husky, casy.

"My parents were schoolteachers. They taught the new writing at the Corporation school. I learned it, but I liked the old writing better. I was interested in writing, in books. In the things my grandparents taught me. They thought I was born to be a maz. Grandmother would say, 'Oh, Kiem, let the child go play!' But Grandfather would want me to stay and learn one more set of characters, and I always wanted to please him. To do better. . . . Grandmother taught me the spoken things, the things children learned of the Telling. But I liked the writing better. I could make it look beautiful. I could keep it. The spoken words just went out like the wind, and you always had to say them all over again to keep them alive. But the writing stayed, and you could learn to make it better. More beautiful."

"So you went to live with your grandparents, to study with them?"

He answered with the same quietness and almost dreamy ease. "When I was a little child, we lived there all together. Then my father became a school administrator. And my mother entered the Ministry of Information. They were transferred to Tambe, and then to Dovza City. My mother had to travel a great deal. They both rose very quickly in the Corporation. They were valuable officials. Very active. My grandparents said it would be better if I stayed home with them, while my parents were moving about and working so hard. So I did."

"And you wanted to stay with them?"

"Oh, yes," he said, with complete simplicity. "I was happy."

The word seemed to echo in his mind, to jar him out of the quietness from which he had been speaking. He turned his head away from Sutty, an abrupt movement that brought vividly to her mind the moment on the street in Okzat-Ozkat when he said to her with passionate anger and pleading, "Do not betray us!"

They sat a while without speaking. No one else was moving about or talking in the Tree Cave. Deep silence in the Lap of Silong.

"I grew up in a village," Sutty said. "With my uncle and aunt. Really my great-uncle and great-aunt. Uncle Hurree was thin and quite dark-skinned, with white bristly hair and eyebrows—terrible eyebrows. I thought he frowned lightning out of them, when I was little. Aunty was a tremendous cook and manager. She could organise anybody. I learned to cook before I learned how to read. But Uncle did teach me, finally. He'd been a professor at the University of Calcutta. A great city in my part of Terra. He taught literature. We had five rooms in the house in the village, and they were all full of books, except the kitchen. Aunty wouldn't allow books in the kitchen. But they were piled all over my room, all around the walls, under the bed and the table. When I first saw the Library caves here, I thought of my room at home."

"Did your uncle teach in the village?"

"No. He hid there. We hid. My parents were hiding in a different place. Lying low. There was a kind of revolution going on. Like yours here, but the other way round. People who . . . But I'd rather listen to you than talk about that. Tell me what happened. Did you have to leave your grandparents? How old were you?"

"Eleven," he said.

She listened. He spoke.

"My grandparents were very active too," he said. His tone had become leaden, labored, though he did not hesitate for words. "But not as loyal producer-consumers. They were leaders of a band of underground reactionary activists. Fomenting cult activities and teaching antiscience. I didn't understand that. They took me to the meetings they organised. I didn't know they were illegal meetings. The umyazu was closed, but they didn't tell me that the police had closed it. They didn't send me to Corporation school. They kept me home and taught me only superstition and deviant morality. Finally my father realised what they were doing. He and my mother had separated. He hadn't been to see me for two years, but he sent for me. A man came. He came at night. I heard my grandmother talking very loudly, angrily. I'd never heard her talk that way. I got up and came into the front room. My grandfather was sitting in his chair, just sitting, he didn't look at me or say anything. Grandmother and a man were facing each other across the table. They looked at me, and then the man looked at her. She said, 'Go get dressed, Azyaru, your father wants you to come see him.' I went and got dressed. When I came out again, they were still just the way they had been, exactly the same: Grandfather sitting like an old, deaf, blind man staring at nothing, and Grandmother standing with her hands in fists on the table, and the man standing there. I began crying. I said, 'I don't want to go, I want to stay here.' Then Grandmother came and held my shoulders, but she pushed me. She pushed me at the man. He said, 'Come on.' And she said, 'Go, Azyaru!' And I . . . went with him."

"Where did you go?" Sutty asked in a whisper.

"To my father in Dovza City. I went to school there." A long silence. He said, "Tell me about . . . your village. Why you were hiding."

"Fair's fair," Sutty said. "But it's a long story."

"All stories are long," he murmured. The Fertiliser had said something like that once. *Short stories are only pieces of the long one,* he had said.

"What's hard to explain is about God, on my world," she said.

"I know God," Yara said.

That made her smile. It lightened her for a moment.

"I'm sure you do," she said. "But what might be hard to understand, here, is what God is, there. Here, it's a word and not much else. In your state theism, it seems to mean what's good. What's right. Is that right?"

"God is Reason, yes," he said, rather uncertainly.

"Well, on Terra, the word has been an enormously important one for thousands of years, among many peoples. And usually it doesn't refer so much to what's reasonable as to what's mysterious. What can't be understood. So there are all kinds of ideas of God. One is that God is an entity that created everything else and is responsible for everything that exists and happens. Like a kind of universal, eternal Corporation."

He looked intent but puzzled.

"Where I grew up, in the village, we knew about that kind of God, but we had a lot of other kinds. Local ones. A great many of them. They all were each other, though, really. There were some great ones, but I didn't know much about them as a child. Only from my name. Aunty explained my name to me once. I asked, 'Why am I Sutty?' And she said, 'Sutty was God's wife.' And I asked, 'Am I Ganesh's wife?' Because Ganesh was the God I knew best, and I liked him. But she said, 'No, Shiva's.'

"All I knew about Shiva then was that he has a lovely white bull that's his friend. And he has long, dirty hair and he's the greatest dancer in the universe. He dances the worlds into being and out of being. He's very strange and ugly and he's always fasting. Aunty told me that Sutty loved him so

much that she married him against her father's will. I knew
that was hard for a girl to do in those days, and I thought she
was very brave. But then Aunty told me that Sutty went back
to see her father. And her father talked insultingly about
Shiva and was extremely rude to him. And Sutty was so angry
and ashamed that she died of it. She didn't *do* anything, she
just *died*. And ever since then, faithful wives who die when
their husbands die are called after her. Well, when Aunty told
me that, I said, 'Why did you name me for a stupid silly
woman like that!'

"And Uncle was listening, and he said, 'Because Sati is
Shiva, and Shiva is Sati. You are the lover and the griever.
You are the anger. You are the dance.'

"So I decided if I had to be Sutty, it was all right, so long
as I could be Shiva too. . . ."

She looked at Yara. He was absorbed and utterly bewildered.

"Well, never mind about that. It is terribly complicated.
But all the same, when you have a lot of Gods, maybe it's easier than having one. We had a God rock among the roots of a
big tree near the road. People in the village painted it red and
fed it butter, to please it, to please themselves. Aunty put
marigolds at Ganesh's feet every day. He was a little bronze
God with an animal nose in the back room. He was Shiva's
son, actually. Much kinder than Shiva. Aunty recited things
and sang to him. Doing pooja. I used to help her do pooja. I
could sing some of the songs. I liked the incense and the

marigolds. . . . But these people I have to tell you about, the people we were hiding from, they didn't have any little Gods. They hated them. They only had one big one. A big boss God. Whatever they said God said to do was right. Whoever didn't do what they said God said to do was wrong. A lot of people believed this. They were called Unists. *One God, one Truth, one Earth*. And they . . . They made a lot of trouble."

The words came out foolish, babyish, primer words for the years of agony.

"You see, my people, I mean all of us on Earth, had done a lot of damage to our world, fought over it, used it up, wasted it. There'd been plagues, famines, misery for so long. People wanted comfort and help. They wanted to believe they were doing something right. I guess if they joined the Unists, they could believe everything they did was right."

He nodded. That he understood.

"The Unist Fathers said that what they called evil knowledge had brought all this misery. If there was no evil knowledge, people would be good. Unholy knowledge should be destroyed to make room for holy belief. They opposed science, all learning, everything except what was in their own books."

"Like the maz."

"No. No, I think that's a mistake, Yara. I can't see that the Telling excludes any knowledge, or calls any knowledge evil, or anything unholy. It doesn't include anything of what Aka has learned in the last century from contact with other civilisations—that's true. But I think that's only because the maz didn't have time to start working all that new information into the Telling before the Corporation State took over as your central social institution. It replaced the maz with bureaucrats, and then criminalised the Telling. Pushed it underground, where it couldn't develop and grow. Called it unholy knowledge, in fact. What I don't understand is why the Corporation thought such violence, such brutal use of power, was necessary."

"Because the maz had had all the wealth, all the power. They kept the people ignorant, drugged with rites and super-stitions."

"But they *didn't* keep the people ignorant! What is the Telling but teaching whatever's known to whoever will listen?"

He hesitated, rubbed his hand over his mouth. "Maybe that was the old way," he said. "Maybe once. But it wasn't like that. In Dovza the maz were oppressors of the poor. All the land belonged to the umyazu. Their schools taught only fos-silised, useless knowledge. They refused to let people have the new justice, the new learning—"

"Violently?"

Again he hesitated.

"Yes. In Belsi the reactionary mob killed two officials of the Corporation State. There was disobedience everywhere. Defiance of the law."

He rubbed his hand hard over his face, though it must have hurt the sore, discolored temple and cheek.

"This is how it was," he said. "Your people came here and they brought a new world with them. A promise of our own world made greater, made better. They wanted to give us that. But the people who wanted to accept that world were stopped, prevented, by the old ways. The old ways of doing everything. The maz mumbling forever about things that happened ten thousand years ago, claiming they knew everything about everything, refusing to learn anything new, keeping people poor, holding us back. They were wrong. They were selfish. Usurers of knowledge. They had to be pushed aside, to make way for the future. And if they kept standing in the way, they had to be punished. We had to show people that they were wrong. My grandparents were wrong. They were enemies of the state. They would not admit it. They refused to change."

He had begun talking evenly, but by the end he was breathing in gasps, staring ahead of him, his hand clenched on the little primer.

"What happened to them?"

"They were arrested soon after I came to live with my father. They were in prison for a year in Tambe." A long pause. "A great number of recalcitrant reactionary leaders were brought to Dovza City for a just public trial. Those who recanted were allowed to do rehabilitative work on the Corporate Farms." His voice was colorless. "Those who did not recant were executed by the producer-consumers of Aka."

"They were shot?"

"They were brought into the Great Square of Justice."
He stopped short.

Sutty remembered the place, a plain of pavement surrounded by the four tall, ponderous buildings housing the
Central Courts. It was usually jammed with stalled traffic
and hurrying pedestrians.

Yara began to talk again, still looking straight ahead at
what he was telling.

"They all stood in the middle of the square, inside a rope,
with police guarding them. People had come from all over to
see justice done. There were thousands of people in the
square. All around the criminals. And in all the streets leading to the square. My father brought me to see. We stood in a
high window in the Supreme Court building. He put me in
front of him so that I could see. There were piles of stones,
building stones from umyazu that had been pulled down, big
piles at the corners of the square. I didn't know what they
were for. Then the police gave an order, and everybody
pushed in toward the middle of the square where the criminals were. They began to beat them with the stones. Their
arms went up and down and . . . They were supposed to
throw the rocks, to stone the criminals, but there were too
many people. It was too crowded. Hundreds of police, and all
the people. So they beat them to death. It went on for a long
time."

"You had to watch?"

"My father wanted me to see that they had been wrong."

He spoke quite steadily, but his hand, his mouth gave him away. He had never left that window looking down into the square. He was twelve years old and stood there watching for the rest of his life.

So he saw his grandparents had been wrong. What else could he have seen?

Again a long silence. Shared.

To bury pain so deep, so deep you never need feel it. Bury it under anything, everything. Be a good son. A good girl. Walk over the graves and never look down. *Keep far the Dog that's friend to men.* . . . But there were no graves. Smashed faces, splintered skulls, blood-clotted grey hair in a heap in the middle of a square.

Fragments of bone, tooth fillings, a dust of exploded flesh, a whiff of gas. The smell of burning in the ruins of a building in the rain.

"So after that you lived in Dovza City. And entered the Corporation. The Sociocultural Bureau."

"My father hired tutors for me. To remedy my education. I qualified well in the examinations."

"Are you married, Yara?"

"I was. For two years."

"No child?"

He shook his head.

He continued to gaze straight ahead. He sat stiffly, not moving. His sleeping bag was tented up over one knee on a kind of frame Tobadan had made to immobilise the knee and

relieve the pain. The little book lay by his hand, JEWEL
FRUITS FROM THE TREE OF LEARNING.

Sutty bent forward to loosen her shoulder muscles, sat up
straight again.

"Goiri asked me to tell you about my world. Maybe I
can, because my life hasn't been so different from yours, in
some ways. . . . I told you about the Unists. After they took
over the government of our part of the country, they started
having what they called cleansings in the villages. It got more
and more unsafe for us. People told us we should hide our
books, or throw them in the river. Uncle Hurree was dying
then. His heart was tired, he said. He told Aunty she should
get rid of his books, but she wouldn't. He died there with
them around him.

"After that, my parents were able to get Aunty and me out of
India. Clear across the world, to another continent, in the
north, to a city where the government wasn't religious. There
were some cities like that, mostly where the Ekumen had
started schools that taught the Hainish learning. The Unists
hated the Ekumen and wanted to keep all the extraterrestrials
off Earth, but they were afraid to try to do it directly. So they
encouraged terrorism against the Pales and the ansible installations and anything else the alien demons were responsible for."

She used the English word *demon*, there being no such
word in Dovzan. She paused a while, took a deep, conscious
breath. Yara sat in the intense silence of the listener.

"So I went to high school and college there, and started

training to work for the Ekumen. About that time, the Ekumen sent a new Envoy to Terra, a man called Dalzul, who'd grown up on Terra. He came to have a great deal of influence among the Unist Fathers. Before very long they were giving him more and more control, taking orders from him. They said he was an angel — that's a messenger from God. Some of them began to say he was going to save all mankind and bring them to God, and so . . ." But there was no Akan word for worship. "They lay down on the ground in front of him and praised him and begged him to be kind to them. And they did whatever he told them to do, because that was their idea of how to do right — to obey orders from God. And they thought Dalzul spoke for God. Or was God. So within a year he got them to dismantle the theocratic regime. In the name of God.

"Most of the old regions or states were going back to democratic governments, choosing their leaders by election, and restoring the Terran Commonwealth, and welcoming people from the other worlds of the Ekumen. It was an exciting time. It was wonderful to watch Unism fall to pieces, crumble into fragments. More and more of the believers believed Dalzul was God, but also more and more of them decided that he was the . . . opposite of God, entirely wicked. There was one kind called the Repentants, who went around in processions throwing ashes on their heads and whipping each other to atone for having misunderstood what God wanted. And a lot of them broke off from all the others and set up some man, a Unist Father or a terrorist leader, as a Savior of their own, and took orders from him. They were all dangerous, they were all violent. The Dalzulites had to protect Dalzul from the anti-Dalzulites. They wanted to kill him. They were always planting bombs, trying suicide raids. All of them. They'd always used violence, because their belief justified it. It told them that God rewards those who destroy unbelief and the unbeliever. But mostly they were destroying each other, tearing each other to pieces. They called it the Holy Wars. It was a frightening time, but it seemed as if there was no real problem for the rest of us — Unism was just taking itself apart.

"Well, before it got as far as that, when the Liberation was just beginning, my city was set free. And we danced in the streets. And I saw a woman dancing. And I fell in love with her."

She stopped.

It had all been easy enough, to this point. This point beyond which she had never gone. The story that she had told only to herself, only in silence, before sleep, stopped here. Her throat began to tighten.

"I know you think that's wrong," she said.

After a hesitation, he said, "Because no children can be born of such union, the Committee on Moral Hygiene declared—"

"Yes, I know. The Unist Fathers declared the same thing. Because God created women to be vessels for men's semen.

But after freedom we didn't have to hide for fear of being sent to revival camps. Like your maz couples who get sent to rehabilitation centers." She looked at him, challenging.

But he did not take the challenge. He accepted what she said and waited, listening.

She could not talk her away around it or away from it. She had to talk her way through it. She had to tell it.

"We lived together for two years," she said. Her voice came out so softly that he turned a little toward her to hear. "She was much prettier than me, and much more intelligent. And kinder. And she laughed. Sometimes she laughed in her sleep. Her name was Pao."

With the name came the tears, but she held them back.

"I was two years older and a year ahead of her in our training. I stayed back a year to be with her in Vancouver. Then I had to go and begin training in the Ekumenical Center, in Chile. A long way south. Pao was going to join me when she graduated from the university. We were going to study together and be a team, an Observer team. Go to new worlds together. We cried a lot when I had to leave for Chile, but it wasn't as bad as we thought it would be. It wasn't bad at all, really, because we could talk all the time on the phone and the net and we knew we'd see each other in the winter, and then after the spring she'd come down and we'd be together forever. We *were* together. We were like maz. We were two that weren't two, but one. It was a kind of pleasure or joy, missing her, because she was there, she was there to miss. And she told me the same thing, she said that when I came back in the winter, she was going to miss missing me. . . ."

She had begun crying, but the tears were easy, not hard. Only she had to stop and sniff and wipe her eyes and nose.

"So I flew back to Vancouver for the holiday. It was summer in Chile, but winter there. And we . . . we hugged and kissed and cooked dinner. And we went to see my parents, and Pao's parents, and walked in the park, where there were big trees, old trees. It was raining. It rains a lot there. I love the rain."

Her tears had stopped.

"Pao went to the library, downtown, to look up something for the examinations she'd be taking after the holiday. I was going to go with her, but I had a cold, and she said, 'Stay here, you'll just get soaked,' and I felt like lying around being lazy, so I stayed in our apartment, and fell asleep.

"There was a Holy War raid. It was a group called the Purifiers of Earth. They believed that Dalzul and the Ekumen were servants of the anti-God and should be destroyed. A lot of them had been in the Unist military forces. They had some of the weapons the Unist Fathers had stockpiled. They used them against the training schools."

She heard her voice, as flat as his had been.

"They used drones, unmanned bombers. From hundreds of kilos away, in the Dakotas. They hid underground and pressed a button and sent the drones. They blew up the college, the library, blocks and blocks of the downtown. Thousands of people were killed. Things like that happened all the time in the Holy Wars. She was just one person. Nobody, nothing, one person. I wasn't there. I heard the noise."

Her throat ached, but it always did. It always would.

She could not say anything more for a while.

Yara asked softly, "Were your parents killed?"

The question touched her. It moved her to a place where she could respond. She said, "No. They were all right. I went to stay with them. After that I went back to Chile."

They sat quietly. Inside the mountain, in the caves full of being. Sutty was weary, spent. She could see in Yara's face and hands that he was tired and still in pain. The silence they shared after their words was peaceful, a blessing earned.

After a long time she heard people talking, and roused herself from that silence.

She heard Odiedin's voice, and presently he spoke outside the tent: "Yara?"

"Come in," Yara said. Sutty pulled the flap aside.

"Ah," said Odiedin. In the weak light of the lantern his dark, high-cheekboned face peering in at them was an amiable goblin mask.

"We've been talking," Sutty said. She emerged from the tent, stood beside Odiedin, stretched.

"I came for your exercises," Odiedin said to Yara, kneeling at the entrance.

"Will he be on his feet soon?" she asked Odiedin.

"Using crutches is hard because of the way his back was hurt," he answered. "Some of the muscles haven't reattached. We keep working on it."

He went into the tent on his knees.

She turned away, then turned back and looked in. To leave without a word, after such a conversation as they had had, was wrong.

"I'll come again tomorrow, Yara," she said. He made some soft reply. She stood up, looking at the cave in the faint glow reflected from the sides of the other tents. She could not see the carving of the Tree on the high back wall, only one or two of the tiny, winking jewels in its foliage.

The Tree Cave had an exit to the outside, not far from Yara's tent. It led through a smaller cave to a short passage that ended in an arch so low that one had to crawl out into the light of day.

She emerged from that and stood up. She had pulled out her dark goggles, expecting to be dazzled, but the sun, hidden all afternoon by the great bulk of Silong, was setting or had set. The light was gentle, with a faint violet tinge. A little snow had fallen during the last few hours. The broad half circle of the cirque, like a stage seen from the backdrop, stretched away pale and untrodden to its outer edge. The air was quiet here under the wall of the mountain, but there at the edge, a hundred meters or so away, wind picked up and dropped the fine, dry snow in thin flurries and skeins, forever restless.

Sutty had been out to the edge only once. The cliff beneath it was sheer, slightly undercut, a mile-deep gulf. It had made her head swim, and as she stood there, the wind had tugged at her, gusting treacherously.

She gazed now over that small, ceaseless dance of the blown snow, across the emptiness of twilit air to Zubuam. The slopes of the Thunderer were vague, pale, remote in evening. She stood a long time watching the light die.

She went to talk with Yara most afternoons now, after she had explored another section of the Library and had worked with the maz who were cataloguing it. She and he never came back directly to what they had told each other of their lives, though it underlay everything they said, a dark foundation.

She asked him once if he knew why the Corporation had granted Tong's request, allowing an offworlder outside the information-restricted, controlled environment of Dovza City. "Was I a test case?" she asked. "Or a lure?"

It was not easy for him to overcome the habit of his official life, of all official lives: to protect and aggrandise his power by withholding information, and to let silence imply he had information even when he didn't. He had obeyed that rule all his adult life and probably could not have broken from it now, if he had not lived as a child within the Telling. As it was, he struggled visibly to answer. Sutty saw that struggle with compunction. Lying here, a prisoner of his injuries, dependent on his enemies, he had no power at all except in silence. To give it up, to let it go, to speak, took valor. It cost him all he had left.

"My department was not informed," he began, then stopped, and began again: "I believe that there have," and finally, doggedly, he started over, forcing himself through the jargon of his calling: "There have been high-level discussions concerning foreign policy for several years. Since an Akan ship is on its way to Hain, and being informed that an Ekumenical ship is scheduled to arrive next year, some elements within the Council have advocated a more relaxed policy. It was said that there might be profit if some doors were opened to an increase of mutual exchange of information. Others involved in decisions on these matters took the view that Corporation control of dissidence is still far too incomplete for any laxity to be advisable. A . . . a form of compromise was eventually attained among the factions of opinion on the matter."

When Yara had run out of passive constructions, Sutty made a rough mental translation and said, "So I was the compromise? A test case, then. And you were assigned to watch me and report."

"No," Yara said with sudden bluntness. "I asked to. Was allowed to. At first. They thought when you saw the poverty and backwardness of Rangma, you'd go back quickly to the city. When you settled in Okzat-Ozkat, the Central Executive didn't know how to exert control without giving offense.

My department was overruled again. I advised that you be sent back to the capital. Even my superiors within the department ignored my reports. They ordered me back to the capital. They won't listen. They won't believe the strength of the maz in the towns and the countryside. They think the Telling is over!"

He spoke with intense and desolate anger, caught in the trap of his complex, insoluble pain. Sutty could think of nothing to say to him.

They sat there in a silence that gradually became more peaceful as they listened and surrendered to the pure silence of the caves.

"You were right," she said at last.

He shook his head, contemptuous, impatient. But when she left, saying she would look in again tomorrow, he muttered, "Thank you, yoz Sutty." Servile address, meaningless ritual phraseology. From the heart.

After that their conversations were easier. He wanted her to tell him about Earth, but it was hard for him to understand, and often, though she thought he did understand, he denied it. He protested: "All you tell me is about destruction, cruel actions, how things went badly. You hate your Earth."

"No," she said. She looked up at the tent wall. She saw the curve in the road just as you came to the village, and the roadside dust she and Moti played in. Red dust. Moti showed her how to make little villages out of mud and pebbles, planting flowers all around them. He was a whole year older than she was. The flowers wilted at once in the hot, hot sun of endless summer. They curled up and lay down and went back into the dark red mud that dried to silken dust.

"No, no," she said. "My world's beautiful beyond telling, and I love it, Yara. I'm telling you propaganda. I'm trying to tell you why, before your government started imitating what we do, they'd have done better to look at who we are. And at what we did to ourselves."

"But you came here. And you had so much knowledge we didn't have."

"I know. I know. The Hainish did the same thing to us. We've been trying to copy the Hainish, to catch up to the Hainish, ever since they found us. Maybe Unism was a protest against that as much as anything. An assertion of our God-given right to be self-righteous, irrational fools in our own particularly bloody way and not in anybody else's."

He pondered this. "But we need to learn. And you said that the Ekumen thinks it wrong to withhold any knowledge."

"I did. But the Historians study the way knowledge should be taught, so that what people learn is genuine knowledge, not a bit here and a bit there that don't fit together. There's a Hainish parable of the Mirror. If the glass is whole, it reflects the whole world, but broken, it shows only fragments, and cuts the hand that holds it. What Terra gave Aka is a splinter of the mirror."

"Maybe that's why the Executives sent the Legates back."

"The Legates?"

"The men on the second ship from Terra."

"Second ship?" Sutty said, startled and puzzled. "There was only one ship from Terra, before the one I came on."

But as she spoke, she remembered her last long conversation with Tong Ov. He had asked her if she thought the Unist Fathers, acting on their own without informing the Ekumen, might have sent missionaries to Aka.

"Tell me about it, Yara! I don't know anything about that ship."

She could see him physically draw back very slightly, struggling with his immediate reluctance to answer. This had been classified information, she thought, known only to the upper echelons, not part of official Corporation history. Though they no doubt assumed *we* knew it.

"A second ship came and was sent back to Terra?" she asked.

"It appears so."

She sent an exasperated silent message at his rigid profile: Oh, don't come the tight-lipped bureaucrat on me *now*! She said nothing. After a pause, he spoke again.

"There were records of the visit. I never saw them."

"What were you told about ships from Terra—can you tell me?"

He brooded a bit. "The first one came in the year Redan Thirty. Seventy-two years ago. It landed near Abazu, on the eastern coast. There were eighteen men and women aboard." He glanced at her to check this for accuracy, and she nodded.

"The provincial governments that were still in power then in the east decided to let the aliens go wherever they liked. The aliens said they'd come to learn about us, and to invite us to join in the Ekumen. Whatever we asked them about Terra and the other worlds they'd tell us, but they came, they said, not as tellers but as listeners. As yoz, not maz. They stayed five years. A ship came for them, and on the ship's ansible they sent a telling of what they'd learned here back to Terra." Again he looked at her for confirmation.

"Most of that telling was lost," Sutty said.

"Did they get back to Terra?"

"I don't know. I left Terra sixty years ago, sixty-one years now. If they got back during the Unist rule, or during the Holy Wars, they might have been silenced, or jailed, or shot. . . . But there was a second ship?"

"Yes."

"The Ekumen sponsored that first ship. But it didn't sponsor another expedition from Terra, because the Unists had taken over. They cut communication with the Ekumen to a bare minimum. They kept closing ports and teaching centers, threatening aliens with expulsion, letting terrorists cripple the facilities, keeping them powerless. If a second ship came from Terra, the Unists sent it. I never heard anything about it, Yara. It certainly wasn't announced to the common people."

Accepting this, he said, "It came two years after the first ship left. There were fifty people on it, with a boss maz, a

leader. His name was Fodderdon. It landed in Dovza, south
of the capital. Its people got in touch with the Corporation
Executives at once. They said Terra was going to give all its
knowledge to Aka. They brought all kinds of information,
technological information. They showed us how we'd have to
stop doing things in the old, ignorant ways and change our
thinking, to learn what they could teach us. They brought
plans, and books, and engineers and theorists to teach us the
techniques. They had an ansible on their ship, so that information could come from Terra as soon as we needed it."

"A great big box of toys," Sutty whispered.

"It changed everything. It strengthened the Corporation
tremendously. It was the first step in the March to the Stars.
Then . . . I don't know what happened. All we were told was
that Fodderdon and the others gave us information freely at
first, but then began to withhold it and to demand an unfair
price for it."

"I can imagine what price," Sutty said.

He looked his question.

"Your immortal part," she said. There was no Akan word
for soul. Yara waited for her to explain. "I imagine he said:
You must believe. You must believe in the One God. You
must believe that I alone, Father John, am God's voice on
Aka. Only the story I tell is true. If you obey God and me,
we'll tell you all the wonderful things we know. But the price
of our Telling is high. More than any money."

Yara nodded dubiously, and pondered. "Fodderdon did

say that the Executive Council would have to follow his orders. That's why I called him a boss maz."

"That's what he was."

"I don't know about the rest. We were told that there were policy disagreements, and the ship and the Legates were sent back to Terra. However. . . . I'm not certain that that's what happened." He looked uncomfortable, and deliberated for a long time over what he was going to say. "I knew an engineer in New Alyuna who worked on the *Aka One*." He meant the NAFAL ship now on its way from Aka to Hain, the pride of the Corporation. "He said they'd used the Terran ship as a model. He may have meant they had the plans for it. But he made it sound as if he'd actually been in the ship. He was drunk. I don't know."

The fifty Unist missionary-conquistadors had very likely died in Corporation labor camps. But Sutty saw now how Dovza itself had been betrayed into betraying the rest of Aka.

It saddened her heart, this story. All the old mistakes, made over and over. She gave a deep sigh. "So, having no way to distinguish Unist Legates from Ekumenical Observers, you've handled us ever since with extreme distrust. . . . You know, Yara, I think your Executives were wise in refusing the bargain Father John offered. Though probably they saw it simply as a power struggle. What's harder to see is that even the gift of knowledge itself had a price attached. And still does."

"Yes, of course it does," Yara said. "Only we don't know what it is. Why do your people hide the price?"

She stared at him, nonplussed.

"I don't know," she said. "I didn't realise . . . I have to think about that."

Yara sat back, looking tired. He rubbed his eyes and closed them. He said softly, "The gift is lightning," evidently quoting some line of the Telling.

Sutty saw beautiful, arching ideograms, high on a shadowy white wall: *the twice-forked lightning tree grows up from earth* She saw Sotyu Ang's worn, dark hands meet in the shape of a mountain peak above his heart. *The price is nothing . . .*

They sat in the silence, following their thoughts.

After a long time, she asked, "Yara, do you know the story about Dear Takieki?"

He stared at her and then nodded. It was a memory from childhood, evidently, that required some retrieval. After a bit longer he said definitely, "Yes."

"Was Dear Takieki really a fool? I mean, it was his mother who gave him the bean meal. Maybe he was right not to give it away, no matter what they offered him."

Yara sat pondering. "My grandmother told me that story. I remember I thought I'd like to be able to walk anywhere, the way he did, without anybody looking after me. I was still little, my grandparents didn't let me go off by myself. So I said he must have wanted to go on walking. Not stay at a farm. And Grandmother asked, 'But what will he do when he runs out of food?' And I said, 'Maybe he can bargain. Maybe he can give the maz some of the bean meal and keep some, and take just a few of the gold coins. Then he could go on walking, and still buy food to eat when winter comes.'"

He smiled faintly, remembering, but his face remained troubled.

It was always a troubled face. She remembered it when it was hard, cold, closed. It had been beaten open.

He was worried for good reason. He was not progressing well with walking. His knee would still not bear weight for longer than a few minutes, and his back injury prevented him from using crutches without pain and risk of further damage. Odiedin and Tobadan worked with him daily, endlessly patient. Yara responded to them with his own dogged patience, but the look of trouble never left him.

———

Two groups had already left the Lap of Silong, slipping away in the dawn light, a few people, a couple of minule, heavyladen. No bannered caravans.

Life in the caves was managed almost wholly by custom and consensus. Sutty had noted the conscious avoidance of hierarchy. People scrupulously did not pull rank. She mentioned this to Unroy, who said, "That was what went wrong in the century before the Ekumen came."

"Boss maz," Sutty said tentatively.

"Boss maz," Unroy confirmed, grinning. She was always tickled by Sutty's slang and her Rangma archaisms. "The

Dovzan Reformation. Power hierarchies. Power struggles. Huge, rich umyazu taxing the villages. Fiscal and spiritual usury! Your people came at a bad time, yoz."

"The ships always come to the new world at a bad time," Sutty said. Unroy glanced at her with a little wonder.

In so far as any person or couple was in charge of things at the Lap of Silong, it was the maz Igneba and Ikak. After general consensus was established, specific decisions and responsibilities were made by them. The order and times at which people were to depart was one such decision. Ikak came to Sutty at dinnertime one night. "Yoz Sutty, if you have no objection, your group will leave four days from now."

"All of us from Okzat-Ozkat?"

"No. You, Maz Odiedin Manma, Long, and Ieyu, we thought. A small group, with one minule. You should be able to travel fast and get down into the hills before the autumn weather."

"Very well, maz," Sutty said. "I hate to leave the books unread."

"Maybe you can come back. Maybe you can save them for our children."

That burning, yearning hope they all shared, that hope in her and in the Ekumen: it frightened Sutty every time she saw its intensity.

"I will try to do that, maz," she said. Then— "But what about Yara?"

"He'll have to be carried. The healers say he won't be

able to walk any long distance before the weather changes. Your two young ones will be in the group with him, and Tobadan Siez, and two of our guides, and three minule with a handler. A large party, but it has to be so. They'll go tomorrow morning, while this good weather holds. I wish we'd known the man would be unable to walk. We'd have sent them earlier. But they'll take the Reban Path, the easiest."

"What becomes of him when you reach Amareza?"

Ikak spread out her hands. "What can we do with him? Keep him prisoner! We have to! He could tell the police exactly where the caves are. They'd send people as soon as they could, plant explosives, destroy it. The way they destroyed the Great Library of Marang, and all the others. The Corporation hasn't changed their policy. Unless *you* can persuade them to change it, yoz Sutty. To let the books be, to let the Ekumen come and study them and save them. If that happened, we'd let him go, of course. But if we do, his own people will arrest and imprison him for unauthorised actions. Poor man, he hasn't a very bright future."

"It's possible that he won't tell the police."

Ikak, surprised, looked her question.

"I know he'd made it a personal mission to find the Library and destroy it. An obsession, in fact. But he . . . He was brought up by maz. And . . ."

She hesitated. She could not tell Ikak his grave-secret any more than she could tell her own.

"He had to become what he was," she said finally. "But I

think all that really makes sense to him is the Telling. I think he's come back to that. I know he feels no enmity toward Odiedin or anybody here. Maybe he could stay with people in Amareza without being kept prisoner. Just keep out of sight."

"Maybe," Ikak said, not unsympathetic but unconvinced. "Except it's very hard to hide somebody like that, yoz Sutty. He has an implanted ZIL. And he was a fairly high official, assigned to watch an Observer of the Ekumen. They'll be looking for him. Once they get him, I'm afraid, whatever he feels, they can make him tell them anything he knows."

"He could stay hidden in a village through the winter, maybe. Not go down into Amareza at all. I will need time, Maz Ikak Igneba—the Envoy will need time—to talk to people in Dovza. And if a ship comes next year, as it's due to, then we can talk on the ansible with the Stabiles of the Ekumen about these matters. But it will take time."

Ikak nodded. "I'll speak with the others about it. We'll do what we can."

Sutty went immediately after dinner to Yara's tent.

Both Akidan and Odiedin were already there, Akidan with the warm clothing Yara would need for the journey, Odiedin to reassure him about making it. Akidan was excited about leaving. Sutty was touched to see how kindly he spoke to Yara, his handsome young face alight. "Don't worry, yoz," he said earnestly, "it's an easy path and we've got a very strong group. We'll be down in the hills in a week."

"Thank you," Yara said, expressionless. His face had closed.

"Tobadan Siez will be with you," Odiedin said.

Yara nodded. "Thank you," he said again.

Kieri arrived with a thermal poncho Akidan had forgotten, and came crowding in with it, talking away. The tent was too full. Sutty knelt in the entrance and put her hand on Yara's hand. She had never touched him before.

"Thank you for telling me what you told me, Yara," she said, feeling hurried and self-conscious. "And for letting me tell you. I hope you—I hope things work out. Goodbye."

Looking up at her, he gave his brief nod, and turned his head away.

She went back to her tent, anxious yet also relieved.

The tent was a mess: Kieri had thrown around everything she owned in preparation for packing it. Sutty looked forward to sharing a tent with Odiedin again, to order, silence, celibacy.

She had spent a long day working on the catalogue, tiring, tricky work with the balky and laborious Akan programs. She went to bed, intending to get up very early and see her friends off. She slept at once. Kieri's return and the fuss of her packing scarcely disturbed her. It seemed about five minutes before the lamp was on again and Kieri was up, dressed, leaving. Sutty struggled out of her sleeping bag and said, "I'll be at breakfast with you."

But when she got to the kitchen, the people of the

departing group weren't there having the hot meal that would start them on their way. Nobody was there but Long, who was on cooking duty.

"Where is everybody, Long?" she asked, alarmed. "They haven't left already, have they?"

"No," Long said.

"Is something wrong?"

"I think so, yoz Sutty." His face was distressed. He nodded toward the outer caves. She went to the entrance that led to them. She met Odiedin coming in.

"What's wrong?"

"Oh Sutty," Odiedin said. He made an incomplete, hopeless gesture.

"What is it?"

"Yara."

"What?"

"Come with me."

She followed him into the Tree Cave. He walked past Yara's tent. There were a lot of people around it, but she did not see Yara. Odiedin strode on through the small cave with a rough floor, and from that to the short passage that led to the outside by the doorway arch they could get through only on hands and knees.

Odiedin stood up just outside it. Sutty emerged beside him. It was far from sunrise still, but the high pallor of the sky seemed wonderfully radiant and vast after the spaceless darkness of the caves.

"See where he went," Odiedin said.

She looked down from the light to where he pointed. Snow lay ankle deep on the floor of the cirque. From the arch where they stood, boot tracks led straight out to the edge and back, tracks of three or four people, she thought.

"Not the tracks," Odiedin said. "Those are ours. He was on hands and knees. He couldn't walk. I don't know how he could crawl on that knee. It's a long way."

She saw, now, the marks in the snow, heavy, dragging furrows. All the boot tracks kept to the left of them.

"Nobody heard him. Sometime after midnight, he must have crept out."

Looking down, quite close to the arch, where the snow was thin on the black rock, she saw a blurred handprint.

"Out there at the edge," Odiedin said, "he stood up. So that he could leap."

Sutty made a little noise. She sank down squatting, rocking her body a little. No tears came, but her throat was tight, she could not breathe.

"Penan Teran," she said. Odiedin did not understand her. "Onto the wind," she said.

"He didn't have to do this." Odiedin's voice was fierce, desolate. "It was wrong."

"He thought it was right," Sutty said.

NINE

THE CORPORATION AIRPLANE that flew her from Soboy
in Amareza to Dovza City gained altitude over the eastern
Headwaters Range. Looking out the small window, due
west, she saw a great, rough, rocky, bulky mountain:
Zubuam. And then, soaring up behind it, the whiteness of
the barrier wall, hiding somewhere in its luminous immen-
sity the cirque and the caves of being. Above the serrate rim
of the barrier, level with her eye, the horn of Silong soared
white-gold against blue. She saw it whole, entire, this one
time. The thin, eternal banner blew northward from the
summit.

The trek south had been hard, two long weeks, on a

good path but with bad weather along much of the way; and she had had no rest in Soboy. The Corporation had their police watching every road out of the Headwaters Range. Officials, very polite, very tense, had met her party just inside the city. "The Observer is to be flown at once to the capital."

She had demanded to speak to the Envoy by telephone, and they had put the call through for her at the airfield. "Come along, as soon as you can," Tong Ov said. "There's been much alarm. We all rejoice at your safe return. Akan and alien alike. Though especially this alien."

She said, "I have to make sure my friends are all right."

"Bring them with you," Tong said.

So Odiedin and the two guides from the village in the foothills west of Okzat-Ozkat were sitting together in the three seats behind hers. What Long and Ieyu made of it all she had no idea. Odiedin had explained or reassured them a little, and they had climbed aboard quite impassively. All four of them were tired, muzzy-headed, worn out.

The plane turned eastward. When she next looked down, she saw the yellow of snowless foothills, the silver thread of a river. The Ereha. Daughter of the Mountain. They followed the silver thread as it broadened and dulled to grey all the way down to Dovza City.

"The base culture, under the Dovzan overlay, is not vertical, not militant, not aggressive, and not progressive," Sutty said. "It's level, mercantile, discursive, and homeostatic. In crisis I think they fall back on it. I think we can bargain with them."

Napoleon Buonaparte called the English a nation of shopkeepers, Uncle Hurree said in her mind. *Maybe not altogether a bad thing?*

Too much was in her mind. Too much to tell Tong; too much to hear from him. They had had little over an hour to talk, and the Executives and Ministers were due to arrive any minute.

"Bargain?" asked the Envoy. They were speaking in Dovzan, since Odiedin was present.

"They owe us," Sutty said.

"Owe us?"

Chiffewar was neither a militant nor a mercantile culture. There were concepts that Chiffewarians, for all their breadth and subtlety of mind, had trouble understanding.

"You'll have to trust me," Sutty said.

"I do," said the Envoy. "But please explain, however cryptically, what this bargain is."

"Well, if you agree that we should try to preserve the Library at Silong. . . ."

"Yes, of course, in principle. But if it involves interference with Akan policy—"

"We've been interfering with Aka for seventy years."

"But how could we arbitrarily refuse them information — since we couldn't undo that first tremendous gift of technological specifics?"

"I think the point is that it wasn't a gift. There was a price on it: spiritual conversion."

"The missionaries," Tong said, nodding. Earlier in their hurried talk, he had shown the normal human pleasure at having his guess confirmed.

Odiedin listened, grave and intent.

"The Akans saw that as usury. They refused to pay it. Ever since then, we've actually given them more information than they asked for."

"Trying to show them that there are less exploitive modes — yes."

"The point is that we've always given it freely, offered it to them."

"Of course," Tong said.

"But Akans pay for value received. In cash, on the spot. As they see it, they didn't pay for all the blueprints for the March to the Stars, or anything since. They've been waiting for decades for us to tell them what they owe us. Till we do, they'll distrust us."

Tong removed his hat, rubbed his brown, satiny head, and replaced the hat a little lower over his eyes. "So we ask them for information in return?"

"Exactly. We've given them a treasure. They have a treasure we want. Tit for tat, as we say in English."

"But to them it's not a treasure. It's sedition and a pile of rotten-corpse superstition. No?"

"Well, yes and no. I think they know it's a treasure. If they didn't, would they bother blowing it up?"

"Then we don't have to persuade them that the Library of Silong is valuable?"

"Well, we do want them to be aware that it's worth fully as much as any information we gave them. And that its value depends on our having free access to it. Just as they have free access to all the information we give them."

"Tat for tit," Tong said, absorbing the concept if not quite the phrase.

"And another thing—very important— That it's not just the books in the Lap of Silong that we're talking about, but all the books, everywhere, and all the people who read the books. The whole system. The Telling. They'll have to decriminalise it."

"Sutty, they're not going to agree to that."

"Eventually they must. We have to try." She looked at Odiedin, who was sitting erect and alert beside her at the long table. "Am I right, maz?"

"Maybe not everything all at once, yoz Sutty," Odiedin said. "One thing at a time. So there's more to keep bargaining with. And for."

"A few gold coins, for some of the bean meal?"

It took Odiedin a while. "Something like that," he said at last, rather dubiously.

"Bean meal?" the Envoy inquired, looking from one to the other.

"It's a story we'll have to tell you," Sutty said.

But the first Executives were coming into the conference room. Two men and two women, all in blue and tan. There were, of course, no formalities of greeting, no servile addresses; but there had to be introductions. Sutty looked into each face as the names were named. Bureaucrat faces. Government faces. Self-assured, smooth, solid. Closed. Endlessly repeatable variations on the Monitor's face. But it was not the Monitor's, it was Yara's face that she held in her mind as the bargaining began.

His life, that was what underwrote her bargaining. His life, Pao's life. Those were the intangible, incalculable stakes. The money burned to ashes, the gold thrown away. Footsteps on the air.